Challenging M

Settlers Book 3

By Tricia McGill

Print ISBNs
BWL Print 978-0-2286-0851-6
LSI/Ingram Print 978-0-2286-0853-0
Amazon Print 978-0-2286-0852-3

BWL Publishing Inc.

Books we love to write ...
Authors around the world.

http://bwlpublishing.ca

Cover art by Michelle Lee

Dedication

To all those invincible settlers who conquered lands and territories against all odds.

Chapter One

Sydney 1840

Tim watched the young ones as they romped around the garden. William, Uncle Remy's eldest at eleven, was chasing his brother Jeremy and the two girls, Emily and tiny Cathy. Cathy at four was a good match for her older siblings and screamed as she joined in the game. Their three dogs thought it a good lark and barked enthusiastically as they ran around in circles. Tim's dog, Bracken, stood back, surveying the younger pups with a regal eye.

Aunt Sara was expecting her fifth offspring in a month or two, so was well on the way to match Mama and Pa's eight children at the rate they were going.

"So, tell me Jo, why are you spending Christmas Day here with us rowdy lot and not with that crusty old Uncle of yours?" Tim asked the small female who sat beside him.

She pulled a face as she chuckled. "Uncle Horace does not believe in festivities. If I stayed at his side on this day, as on any other, he would ask why I am not out with my friends." She touched her pert nose with a finger. "I do believe he will spend the day at his account books. His favourite pastime in the whole world is counting money, and the awful truth of it is he has not one whit or notion of what to do with it."

"He treats you kindly though, doesn't he?" Tim often worried about the chit. Bushrangers killed her parents while they mined out Bathurst way just before last Christmas, hence she now lived with her one and only relative here in town. Tim's kind-hearted sister Annie, being of a similar age, had befriended Jo when she was brought into Bathurst by the local military after the killings. Luckily, Jo had time to find a hiding place, so escaped murder or worse at the hands of the ruffians who were after gold. Lord only knew how horrifying the experience must have been for the girl.

Mama and Pa offered her a home with them, but it was considered only right she go to live with her only relative. Mama and Annie ensured she had Uncle Remy and Aunt Sara's address, and of course, Aunt Sara welcomed Jo into her home whenever she wished and had even given her employment at the thriving emporium she inherited from her father on his death.

"Well, I have a notion he would rather not have me in his home." She shrugged. "But I am fed well, and he gives me a small allowance for my personal needs, so I cannot complain. I am not the type of person who pines for pretty clothes and fripperies, so I presume he is prepared to put up with me—if not show me tenderness." She set a small hand on Tim's arm. "Do not misunderstand me. I am happy. I can come and go as I please. There are many other young women of my age here in town who are harangued daily by their mothers to find a suitor, especially one with means to provide them with a large home and all that goes with it."

Tim had wondered at her lack of self-importance. Unlike most other girls here in Sydney Town she never primped or put on airs. She dressed quite plainly in fact and was happier romping about with the young ones rather than sitting around looking pretty and simpering. "Tell me something else, when you have such a pretty name as Josephine, why do you insist we call you Jo?"

She laughed at that. "My parents were not strict and let me run wild as a child. My father often said I was more like the son he wished he had instead of a girl. It was he who called me Jo, and it seems to have stayed with me. I spent most of my childhood at the mining site, so was used to the company of young men and boys." She pushed her long tresses back over her shoulder and smiled. "Papa said it was a safeguard. Some of the men were unruly and some convicts, and he thought it better if they regarded me as one of them rather than a prissy miss who craved attention."

That she certainly did not do. In fact, Tim had a feeling she had no idea of her attractiveness. With silky dark tresses reaching almost to her middle and a slender litheness that came from her love of activity, she was altogether a comely lass. This mane was secured back today by a simple ribbon, likely because of the heat. She often complained that it was a menace. Privately he hoped she never had it shorn.

Aunt Sara appeared with a tray of drinks and cakes and the young ones all gathered noisily around, arguing over who should be first to be served. Tim rose and stretched just as Uncle Remy came from the house. His mother's brother was a handsome man with dark complexion and a mass of reddish hair that came from his Spanish father. His brothers Carlos and Bob, who still worked alongside Tim's father on their extensive sheep property in Bathurst, shared the same colouring.

Tim had inherited Pa's colouring. Everyone called his father Tiger. The story went that an old sailing codger of his long ago tagged him so because of his mane of golden hair. Tim always wanted to be dark like his Uncles Remy, Bob and Carlos—their foreign appearance possessed a mysterious quality. Mind you, he was glad his father's good looks and build had passed on to his sons. Vain of him, he knew, but he liked the attention he received from the unmarried women about town, and even some of the married ladies sometimes gave him the eye. Josephine was one of the few females who seemed unaffected by his charm and appearance. Tim wasn't wholly sure if that irked him or not.

"Let's walk for a bit," Uncle Remy said with a small wave of his hand. "After all the food we have eaten we need the exercise."

Their garden was now set out so that the children had plenty of room to frolic to their heart's content. The few trees they planted on coming here eight years ago were flourishing alongside the giant eucalyptus that had most probably offered its shade for many years.

They walked in companionable silence for a few minutes before his uncle said, "So, Tim, what have you decided? I received a letter from your Ma and Pa as you did in the last mail that came back from Bathurst along with the wagons the other day, and both your parents seem unimpressed by your decision to take off into the relatively unknown part of the country. From what I have gathered from my colleagues, the road to Port Philip can barely be called a road at this current stage."

Tim chuckled softly. "Hmm, Pa said almost as much to me. He cannot understand why I would forsake good employment with the Government to go a wandering, as he called it. As I told you, I broached the subject while celebrating my birthday with them in September." Tim shrugged. "I often think that Pa has completely forgotten he did the same thing when he decided to up us all to travel across the mountains when I was just a young 'un. He says that was different, they travelled over there to seek fresh pastures for their sheep, but he cannot see why I should wish to desert a safe career to wander—as he called it. And, he also seems unaware that great advances are being made to the road all the time."

"I guess in a way he is right, Tim. Your position at Government House brings you in contact with surveyor's reports, so you more than anyone must know the road south is still in a sorry state. Last I heard, beyond Yass is still more or less uncharted territory, populated by a rag-tag motley of settlers with neither church nor schools for their offspring, who run wild. Surely, you cannot be in search of riches, for you are more likely to be robbed along the way and lose everything rather than gain a fortune. The bushrangers are not so busy these days, but I heard only recently of a man and his family being robbed at gunpoint by these ruffians not far from the cities' outer borders. The population now might consist of mainly freemen willing to work for gain, but the world will always have those on the lookout for easy profit."

Tim knew well of his uncle's days on the road and how he had been accidentally caught up in the shenanigans of a violent gang of robbers while crossing the mountains years ago, so his opinion would be coloured by this experience. Even so, things had improved in the intervening years. How could he put into words his desire to break free, to seek a life of his own beyond the confines of his family? As much as he loved them all, since leaving Kings School it seemed his life had become dull and boring through no choice of his own. The highlight of the last few years had been his annual visits to Bathurst to catch up with Mama and Papa and their large clan. His qualifications at the end of his schooling had been such that a position was found for him almost instantly.

"Do you recall my ambition when I arrived here in town with you as a twelve-year-old, Uncle Remy?" he asked, stopping to lean against the gum tree. He bent to scratch behind Bracken's ear. His dog was a hound of good breeding and the most intelligent dog he had ever owned and followed Tim slavishly.

Uncle Remy shook his head. "You had a few, from memory. But most were boyish fancies, and these seldom come to fruition, for any of us."

"Not so. My main ambition was to work in animal husbandry if not science of some sort. As you recall I used to embarrass Aunt Sara by expounding on my vast knowledge of the breeding habits of certain animals. Here in this country we have an extraordinary array of unusual species. I would have liked nothing more than to work alongside Joseph Banks who journeyed here with Captain Cook."

Uncle Remy laughed. "Yes, I remember well." He placed a hand on Tim's arm. "There are other factors that worry your father in particular, Tim. There is much unrest among the natives and the landowners. Since the abolition of transportation from Britain, many free settlers have taken off to settle on virgin lands down south. This has caused disruptions in many places as they cross land the natives see as rightfully theirs."

"I am well aware of this Uncle Remy, and between you and me I am on the side of the natives. This has been their country since time began and they have their own sets of rules. I find their beliefs and practices fascinating. Their connection with the land is something I would like to learn more about."

"Hmm, and well you might, young lad, but believe me they see us as invaders, and perhaps we are. Since Governor Burke's proclamation that no one owned this land before the Crown took possession of it, matters have worsened." Uncle Remy looked to the house as Aunt Sara called. "Come, I think we are being summoned." He grinned.

He walked off, but Tim lingered. He knelt to stroke Bracken's ear as Josephine approached. "Can I come with you?" she asked.

"And just where do you wish to accompany me, young Jo?" Straightening, he began to stroll towards the house with her at his side.

"Rude of me, I know, but I couldn't help but overhear your discussion with your uncle." She lowered her voice and bent closer. Tim caught a scent of lavender. Carefree of feminine ways she might be, but she smelt as good as any young miss. "I shouldn't sound so ungrateful, as your aunt ensured I had employment in her emporium when I arrived here in town, but the tasks are so tedious. I am bored. I thought of running off and making my own way in the world." Her face grew comical as she wrinkled her pert nose.

"Silly chit. Don't you dare even contemplate such a rash move," he scolded. "You are not naïve, I think, and must know the dangers that exist beyond the sanctuary of a safe home. Anyway, I could not consider taking you along on such a dangerous journey."

She made an unladylike noise. "Don't you dare suggest I could not cope with such a journey. I roved free for all of my childhood while my parents worked their mine. I told you, my father treated me more as a son than a daughter. A wizened old woman, who took care of the cooking, also saw to my schooling. Matilda was governess to a family in England before being transported for thieving—a false charge according to her. She had gained her ticket of leave and accompanied my parents on their quest for gold. She was very knowledgeable." A deep sadness clouded her eyes, as she said, "Poor Matilda was slain on that terrible day."

"It must have been awful for you." She seldom spoke about the tragedy, so they had no idea how deeply she felt about losing not only her parents, but people who were like family to her.

Her shoulders lifted as she sighed. "Awful yes, but my father taught me to be strong and my mother taught me to be brave." Her face brightened. "Always look to the future, he advised, there is no room in life for regrets."

"Wise words." Tim had been curious about her schooling, as according to Aunt Sara she did well at the emporium, coping with any problem that arose. To change to a more cheerful subject he said, "My aunt would not wish to lose you. She assures me you will make manager one day soon."

"Nonsense." Jo waved that suggestion aside. "The husband and wife who presently run the store do so adequately and will be doing so for at least another twenty years. I do not wish to wait around that long. And anyway, I have dreams and plans." She touched her nose with a finger.

"So tell me, Jo, just what plans are these—apart from thinking to accompany me on a trek that may take months?"

"Well, to be honest, the idea only occurred to me while I was listening in to your conversation with your uncle, but I wish to travel. This country is huge…" She spread her arms wide. "And so much of it has never been trod upon by a white man. If I had been born a man, I would have joined one of the surveying teams, preferably one such as that led by Gregory Blaxland, William Wentworth or William Lawson." Her smile held a wistful quality. "Imagine what it would be like to come upon a river or stretch of land that only the natives knew about."

Tim had to admit her dreams were not so different to his own, but for fear of encouraging her he wasn't about to admit such. The children shouting for him to come inside cut their conversation short. As they reached the doorway, Tim stopped her with a touch on the arm.

"Jo, you are at an age for marriage, and by now should be contemplating the beaux of your choice, not thinking of gallivanting off around the country in search of green pastures—leave that to us men."

The sound she made would have been unacceptable in polite company. Tim suppressed a smile. "Have you looked around here lately at the young males? The men who seek my company are simpering fools. Anyway, I am but seventeen and am not about to consider marriage, and what goes with it, for quite a few years yet." She arched a brow. "Now that's an idea, I could marry you, and then you would have no qualms about me tagging along with you on your travels."

Tim laughed aloud. "Wench, you are incorrigible. I am but twenty-one and most certainly not ready for marriage either." One thing was for sure, a wife such as Josephine would definitely never be boring.

Chapter Two

April 1841

"Uncle Carlos! When did you arrive?" Tim discarded his satchel and went to put his arms around his uncle. "Welcome."

Uncle Carlos pulled free and placed a hand on Tim's shoulder. "The wagons pulled into town just after daybreak. I have been dozing most of the day. As you know, the journey across the mountains is anything but enjoyable, and I am getting old."

Tim gave him a playful shove. "Rubbish—you're but fifteen years my senior and in your prime, and you know it. So, to another question, why are you here? I'm certain, knowing my Pa, that this is not simply a family visit." The last letter Tim received from his parent stressed in detail how absurd his father thought his plan to set out towards Port Philip.

After a few days of extreme heat, the weather had blessedly cooled, so they both went to sit on chairs on the back verandah. After Aunt Sara had been out to question what they would like to drink, and gone back inside to take care of that, Uncle Carlos said, "Of course, he is not happy, but…" He shrugged. "He realises you share his blood so can easily understand your desire to seek fresh pastures. What your mother especially is fretting about is the unrest that is rife among the farmers and natives."

Tim sighed. "We must face the fact that there will always be misunderstandings between the settlers and them. As I keep trying to explain to everyone, they have as much right to hang onto their land as we do ours."

Uncle Carlos leant forward, elbows on his knees. "Tiger did not want to see me leave, but as I stressed, he has our brother Bob there along with him. Our Bob took to farming like a duck to water. He thrives on the hard work. Ginger is still able to work as hard as any younger man, and Mole, who is as old as the hills, is still the best shepherd who ever rounded up his sheep."

"Thank you." Tim nodded to Aunt Sara's maid, as she set a tray containing their drinks on the small table. "My father has been lucky," he said. "A lot of farmers were not as lucky with their choice of helpers." Ginger had been with him forever it seemed, as had old Mole.

"Between you and me, Tim, I was ready for a change. After your visit last year when you started talking about a journey, I began to think that it was time for me to make a change. I do admit that Tiger was pleased to hear I was thinking of accompanying you, but this is wholly my decision, I can assure you." He patted Tim's knee. "After all, as you say, I am in my prime, and so far, haven't found myself a woman I fancy to take as a wife. The choice is limited in Bathurst." He grinned mischievously. "Not that there have not been a few who would be willing, I know. However, my gut tells me the time is right for me to make changes. Now, I am presuming you have no objections to me accompanying you."

Tim laughed. "Nothing would please me more—just one thing. As we are to be travelling companions perhaps it is time I dropped your title and called you Carlos?"

"Perfect. Now, Tim, bring me up to date on what level you have reached with your planning? Are you forming your own travelling group, or do you intend going along with one of the bullock teams?"

"My position at the government offices has entitled me to information I would not otherwise have known. I have been fortunate as, working in the survey office, I have been privy to facts about some of the smaller exploration teams that have set out in the past year. My superior applauded my decision." Tim laughed. "I do not doubt he will be glad to see my back, as I have talked about nothing but setting out on my adventurous trip for the past year. I have arranged to travel along with a bullocky named Jacko—a reliable Irishman who has spent his life on the road, and he has agreed that we accompany him to his furthest destination, which is Yass. Beyond that we are on our own it seems."

Carlos looked doubtful at that. "Hmm, are you certain this is wise? Last I heard civilisation ends at Yass, and beyond that the road becomes little more than a bush track."

Tim waved a hand. "Since the first settlers arrived, we have been going beyond the well-trodden tracks. We might prove lucky and meet up with another team of bullockies heading south from Yass. Anyway, what about the hazards Pa and Mama faced when they crossed the mountains on a barely existing road?"

"And from what I have heard, there were more than a few hazards and disasters, young Tim."

"Just so. My half brother died of snakebite on the way over, when he was barely out of babyhood, and his father fell to his death. We all face risks every day in life. Only last week a woman was run down by a stray wagon when the driver lost control. How boring life would be if we never took risks?"

"Seems to me you have the right set of mind for the adventure. So, what date has this Jacko given you for his departure?"

"You timed your arrival perfectly, Carlos. One of the main factors in choosing this bullocky was the weather. We thought it best to set out when the days were growing cooler, but not so late in the year that we encountered snow and cold weather in some inland places. Jacko informed me that it can get quite cold overnight in many high points along the way. So, we leave in two weeks." Tim rubbed his hands together, finished his drink, and stood. "There is still much to do."

* * *

The cattle market was noisy to extreme, and they could hear the bellows of the oxen as they passed Carters Barracks and the Government Paddocks on the edge of town. Unfortunately, the weather had heated again after the cool break, making the stink heavy on the nose. They were not the only ones leaving today—another two wagons were setting out and one had newly arrived even though it was barely past daybreak.

"I recall meeting up with Remy here all those years ago, and the joy we felt at catching up with each other after time apart," Carlos said as they passed into the yards.

"A lot has happened to both of you since then." Tim whistled to his hound, Bracken, who was happily sniffing about the legs of the oxen. The dog obediently returned to his horse's side.

"And more to Remy than me. But he has come through and remains a good man at heart."

"True. And he and Aunt Sara have treated me as another of their sons since they brought me back with them as a raw twelve-year-old, so that I could attend Kings School." Tim sighed. "Aunt Sara shed a few tears at our farewell, but I got the distinct feeling that Uncle Remy would have liked to accompany us." He hailed Jacko as he caught sight of him tending his bullocks, and they headed towards him.

Tim dismounted and tied his horse and the packhorse to a rail, and Carlos did the same. They had decided that two packhorses would likely be one too many but when Jacko assured Tim that it might be difficult to acquire fresh horses along the way, had changed plans, considering it better to be safe than sorry. His original plan had been to hire a man to accompany him, but when Carlos arrived, that plan was scrapped. If they found the need for another pair of hands, no doubt they could pick up a willing worker along the way.

"Nice morning for it," Jacko shouted as he hailed them. Tim had already introduced him to Carlos when they met up last week to make final plans. "We'll be off as soon as I get old Daisy here in her harness. She can be worse to handle than any of my women." His roar of laughter rang out above the din, as he tugged at his chest-long matted beard.

Tim chuckled. Although the bullock drivers were as hard as iron and used the strongest language imaginable, it was well known that they treated their animals with the highest regard. To lose a bullock was to them worse than losing a leg or arm—or seemingly a lady-friend.

Other men and their horses milled around now as Tim and Carlos made a final check of their horses. Tim looked towards the road as another two riders arrived, along with a pack animal. There was something familiar about the front rider and he took his hat off and scratched his head as he tried to fathom where he would have met this fellow. As they drew closer Tim gasped, "Lord above, it's Jo! What the hell is the tyke doing here?"

"Do you know him?" Carlos asked as he unbent from checking hooves. "He's young, and not bad to look on. What is such a young fella doing travelling with only a black sidekick for company?"

"That, Carlos, is no him. That is a stubborn female who thinks she can defy me and come along with us."

"Female?" Carlos looked as confused as Tim felt. "But women ride side-saddle do they not? And usually wear skirts if I am not mistaken."

"Normal women, yes, but believe me this one is not normal." Josephine and her companion stopped a few paces away, and the chit had the audacity to grin. "I told you, young Madam, that this is no journey for a scrap of a girl. And just who have you dragged into your artful scheme?"

"This is Billy. He worked for my father. Believe me, he will be no trouble," she said, completely ignoring his reprimand. She bent to pat Bracken's head when the dog put his front paws on her foot in the stirrup, the better to greet her with a lick and a small woof.

"It's not him I am worried about, but you Madam. I told you in no uncertain terms, Jo, that this was no short day trip and there is certainly no place for a female of good breeding where we are going. You can turn around right now and take those animals back to your uncle who you no doubt stole them from."

That seemed to make her indignant. "These are my animals, I assure you, and Billy came along of his own free will. He wants to track down his family if he can so he can return to where he rightfully belongs." She took off her hat and shook her hair—hair that barely covered her ears.

"You've cut off your locks," Tim said, before realising that was the stupidest remark he could have made, and of no importance to the subject at hand.

She plonked the wide-brimmed hat back on and flicked a stray strand back from her face. "I considered it more admirable shorter for our journey."

"Our journey? Since when did this become something you shared in?" He was running out of suitable arguments. But then a thought struck. "Did your uncle agree to this?"

"You may not believe this, but he couldn't care a fig one way or the other. He was not worried about Billy tagging along, as all he needs is the one handler for his carriage and two horses. And to be honest, he seemed happy he had fewer mouths to feed and one less female to worry about." She waved a gloved hand. "And another thing—Billy never forgot his native tongue, despite being dragged away from his family when he was a child. That could be of use to you, do you not think?"

Jacko let out a roar and shouted, "Away my fellows," to his six oxen.

Tim had one more card up his sleeve. He'd spent enough time around animals to know how the female body worked. It was not the sort of thing one discussed with a lady—but then again, she was no well-bred woman, so he said in a soft voice. "Females have habits and needs that we men do not have to endure. Are you certain you wish to be the only woman amongst so many men?" Apart from him and Carlos, Jacko had three sidekicks, all mature men who had likely been on the road most of their life.

At least that made her blush—or perhaps it was the heat making her cheeks rosy. "As I have told you on numerous occasions, I was brought up among miners and convicts for most of my young life. My mother taught me how to behave among men, so have no fear I will not embarrass you." She tossed her head. "And I have been riding astride all my life," she added, as if that settled it.

Carlos had been standing back watching. The small grin on his face annoyed Tim, who saw nothing amusing about this and was at a loss now what to do. The chit had no doubt thought this all through. Short of dragging her back to her uncle's home—and then having to gallop his horse back to catch up with Jacko—there was little he could think of to deter her. "Be it on your own head," he muttered as he mounted. "And don't blame me if you get down the road a bit and decide you have made the wrong decision. I will not accompany you back, no matter what happens."

She snorted. "You are more likely to be the one to realise you are not man enough for such a journey," she had the nerve to respond, as she kicked her horse up alongside his.

"Insolent woman," he said, asking, "Does your friend speak our language?" So far, Billy had not spoken a word.

"Of course. Do not misunderstand, native he might be, and most white men look down on him, but he knows more about life than most ordinary men. That is another thing that will be of infinite use to us, he knows an awful lot about plants and has an inbuilt connection with the land, something you or I will never possess. We will never starve as long as he is here to help us."

Tim had no answer for that, as he knew it was likely true. One thing he found disconcerting was that the settlers as a whole failed to value the worth of the natives whose skills had been handed down through countless generations spent traversing this land. Fanciful it might be, but this was a sinful wrong that he desired be put to rights one day. Many settlers failed to understand that they could not continue to farm as they did in their country of birth where the climate was far different to here in this oft-times dry and dusty land. Many had already learnt the hard way, suffering through fires and dry seasons.

They continued in silence until the cavalcade left the outskirts of town behind. Carlos kept aside of Jacko who sat atop his wagon, and the two were deep in conversation. Tim had a feeling that the bullock driver was regaling his uncle with raucous tales of his travels by the sound of their merry laughter. Jo seemed to take a great interest in the many varieties of birds. When they spied a mob of kangaroos off to the side, she turned in her saddle to watch them as they bounded away.

"It seems those creatures are unknown back where our parents came from. This is odd is it not?" he asked, more to make conversation than anything else.

She smiled. "Rather than watch it starve, my mother often reared a young one if its mother was shot for food. She said that most of the animals in this land are unknown elsewhere. Billy has many stories he can tell of where the animals came from. Each billabong and hill you see has a myth attached to it. White men only look on the land as something to be cultivated and ruined for their own advantage, whereas the natives are at one with it and it controls their life."

He'd had many conversations in the past with Jo, but now Tim was seeing another side to her. Her beliefs so mirrored his own he was startled. "I think your mother was a wise woman, was she not?" he asked.

A small smile of reminiscence crossed her face as she nodded. "My father also was a knowledgeable man." She sighed deeply. "If they had not been transported for stupid petty thievery the pair would have ended up in a much different situation."

"So, how is it they became miners if they were intelligent well-educated folk?"

"That is the sorriest part of their tale. Father became obsessed by the stupid idea of gaining wealth the easy way." The small sound of disgust she made displayed her opinion of this foolhardy venture. "As my mother told me, he met a man while working out at the sheep-yards, and this person convinced my father that all he had to do was go off into the mountains and gold was waiting there for any man with the strength and will to search for it." She shrugged. "So as soon as both gained their tickets of leave, off he dragged her. I think she adored him, and that is why she endured such a hard life. I will never make the mistake of loving a man with such brainless ideas."

Tim let out a harrumph. "Foolish girl. I have been told that love is blind, and when it strikes there is little you can do but go along with it. She gave birth to you and obviously loved you even though she let you run wild and behave more like a young larrikin than a respectable woman of breeding."

"Hah! No thank you—I would never wish to be a primping simpering female of breeding. Have you observed how the so-called high-class ladies behave in town? And their Mamas!" She made a rude sound in her throat. "When I decide to marry, supposing I ever do, it will be with the man of my choice and not some moneybags chosen by a parent—or in my case, an uncle who cares little for me and more for amassing wealth. Why, he was already suggesting likely husbands for me as soon as I passed my seventeenth birthday. All of them many years my senior." Another rude sound emphasised her opinion of that.

"Well, you are a free woman now it appears—and soon will be far away from him and any decisions he could have made for your future," Tim said. What a sad life she had endured to date, even though her parents obviously loved her in some strange way. "It must have been horrific for you when they were killed." Tim knew she did not like talking about that fateful day but she seemed in a talkative mood right now, so he ventured the question.

For a while, she stared into the distance without speaking. "I still wake at night with nightmares," she said. "Mother heard the gang before she saw them drawing near and told me to hide. There was always a fear of being robbed out there, and so she taught me well. I lay securely in my hiding place and heard my father pleading with the bushrangers, not for himself but for Mama. Their laughter rang out as they shot him and then when mother ran at them, they shot her. A couple of the miners had already run off, but they shot the ones that remained."

Tim was at a loss what to say. No wonder the chit was hardened. He was not about to mention it, but her mother was lucky not to suffer assault by the gang, or worse. They could have dragged her off into the hills. Other women had suffered this fate at the hands of ruffians.

"They ransacked the surrounding area and pulled down our tents and scattered our belongings around the clearing." She waved a hand as if it did not bother her—but he knew that of course it did. She leaned closer and said in a whisper, "They never found all the gold. As I said, my father had brains and was not some fly-by-night miner who boasted about every new find. My mother ensured I would be well looked after in the event of their death and told me where to find their hoard."

Tim stared at her. "You are telling me that you secured some of the gold and brought it back to town when the military brought you to your uncle's house. So where is it now?"

A finger touched her nose as she revealed, "I am not stupid. I have to admit that the manager at the Savings Bank was astonished when I arrived and ordered he open an account for me. Of course he wanted my guardian's approval, but I was not about to let my uncle anywhere near my inheritance."

"So, who stepped forward as your guarantor? It is unlikely a lass of your age would be able to open a bank account."

"I know—I am of marriageable age, but not considered a woman who can control her own property. To be honest it disgusted me."

Tim could well understand her indignation. He was still digesting her revelations. Stupidly he thought she had arrived at her uncle's home a penniless waif in need of shelter. "I am presuming you found someone to assist you."

Her small laugh had Carlos looking their way. Since the sun rose higher in the sky, the day had warmed considerably. Tim wondered if the heat was worrying Jo but was not about to change the subject to ask her.

"Of course. Your kind Uncle Remy and his beautiful Sara stepped up for me, else I would have been in a pickle indeed."

That amazed Tim so much his head went back in shock. "You mean to tell me they knew this entire tale yet never mentioned a word of it?"

"Why would they? My affairs are of no importance to anyone," she proclaimed.

"Fair enough." Tim didn't know whether to feel upset he was left out of her secret or feel admiration for the chit. "So all your wealth now resides in a bank in Sydney Town?"

After another merry laugh, she bent close again and whispered, "I have enough to cover my costs along the way, have no fear."

"You have? But where have you secreted gold? Is it about your person or within your packs?" He glanced back at Billy who looked to be asleep atop his mount. "Tell me you have not secreted it in the baggage you carry."

That brought another look of indignation from her. "You think me an imbecile?" she almost spluttered. "I sold most of my gold—too many greedy hands would have been after it. No, if I decide to stay at Port Philip the bank have instructions to have my account transferred at my word. I have sufficient to see me through the journey."

Jacko's shout of, "River ahead. We rest the animals here," stopped Tim from further comment. Her revelations had stunned him beyond belief, forcing him to see her in a very different light. He had totally miscalculated her—far from being a young tearaway with little breeding, there was no doubt that her parents had taught her well.

Now he was left to wonder why her father chose mining over more substantial employment in town—the man was without doubt very intelligent to ensure this snip of a lass gained so much knowledge. Many other girls of her age would have no idea of banking, as their fathers managed their affairs and once married it would be left to their husbands to ensure their dowry was taken care of.

He wasn't about to ask just where she had hidden some of her wealth, but knew women wore various odd garments beneath their outer clothing. He could never see Jo stooping to wear such a contraption as a corset. From what his sister Annie divulged on his last visit home—such garments were a curse on womanhood, and she refused point blank ever to wear one, no matter how Mama badgered her.

His minimal contact with females' underclothes consisted of a few visits to a brothel, and he doubted very much that the clothing worn by the harlots there was a good example of what decent women wore. The first time, Tim went with a schoolmate of similar disposition, and the pair of them were so red-faced afterwards they could barely talk about it. It seemed that the older boys who had encouraged them to go there with them thought it a huge laugh. Tim went along with their banter rather than show his inexperience.

His next visit was with a fellow from his place of employment, and was more to satisfy his curiosity, for he guessed there had to be more to be gained from coupling. This fellow took Tim to a house of ill repute, where the rather large female in charge advised him an older woman would best serve his needs. This one wore a dirty chemise and smelt of whiskey and lord only knew what else, and claimed, "My God, lad, you should have come to see me years ago. Many lads are barely off their mother's tits before they come a' running to taste the delights of the likes of me." But he had to admit she knew her trade, and it was fine as long as he kept his eyes closed and did not inhale too often.

The men he worked alongside made regular visits to the women at this house, but Tim knew enough of diseases passed on from animal to animal to know that a man could surely end up with some awful disease after copulating with such women who could have shared their bodies with many a foreign seaman passing through. He was more prudent and craved a love such as his parents, or his Uncle

Remy and Aunt Sara shared. All had gone through many heartaches along their path to finding happiness, and deep down, Tim hoped he would meet the perfect woman—one he could love without reservation.

By its position in the sky, Tim guessed it to be near midday, so they had been in the saddle for a few hours. He had to applaud the little Madam for ensuring the time passed quickly and wondered what other secrets she would reveal before this journey was over. Bracken lapped until full in the river, went off to cock his leg up a tree and then flopped down in the shade.

After ensuring the horses were all watered and secured, Tim looked about. Jacko had chosen the spot well. The small scattering of trees gave shelter from the sun. Jo was sauntering off towards a group of shrubs a distance away, Billy a few paces behind her. "Watch for snakes," Tim called.

She waved a hand over a shoulder. "Billy will watch out for me," she shouted back, before disappearing behind a small bush. Jacko and his men were not so shy, and most were relieving themselves in full view of the others. Carlos and Tim walked off a bit to take care of business.

"You and the chit seem to be finding plenty to talk about," Carlos commented with a chuckle as they strolled back. "So it seems she will accompany us all the way to Port Philip, hey?"

"Well, it appears to be the decision she has made, Carlos. I have to admit she has the cheek of the devil, and if anyone can survive the journey it will be her."

When she returned, she washed her hands and face in the river before taking a small bundle from Billy, who then sat with his back against a tree trunk. She unwrapped slabs of bread and cheese and asked, "Would you share with us, Tim and Carlos? I am afraid I did not think to bring more, so cannot offer to the other men—who seem to be managing quite well with their provisions."

One of the men had a small fire going and the billycan was already boiling. One dread Tim had was that Jacko and his side-kicks might take to the grog, but they seemed to be satisfied with the tea made over the fire—for now.

"How do you fare?" Tim asked, as he took a chunk of bread and cheese from Jo. "Are your legs coping with so many hours in the saddle?"

She nodded, as her mouth was full, but as she finished chewing, she said, "Oh yes, my father always boasted that I was born on a horse's back. I doubt that was altogether true, but I certainly spent many hours riding. There was little else to do once the chores were finished and my schooling done for the day." She handed a small piece of cheese to Bracken who then lay at her side, probably in the hope of cadging more.

It occurred to Tim that she was most likely fitter for this trip than he was. Although he rode every weekend, often far into the outskirts of the town in search of the many animals that roamed free, his week had mostly been spent in boring tasks in an enclosed space at Government House. Perhaps he should have ridden more to prepare himself—but he would never admit such to her. "And what else did you do to pass the time?" he asked. "Were your parents not worried by you riding out alone in such dangerous territory?"

"I was never alone. Billy here accompanied me, and to answer your question, I like to sketch—especially birds. This land abounds with beautiful specimens, creatures that most folk rarely take notice of." Her face saddened. "And to be honest, my parents most likely thought I would be safer away from the mine—a suspicion that proved true."

"Five minutes," Jacko shouted, putting an end to any further conversation as they all prepared to move off.

Chapter Three

There was little doubt that the grass grew more plentiful the more miles they put between them and the town. “It is easy to see why so many decide to leave the town and head to finer pastures,” Carlos commented, nodding towards a flock of sheep they could just see on the horizon. “There is land for the taking, and many are taking it.”

“Well, perhaps not taking it as such. Last I heard, most squatters could claim as much as they wanted but only on the condition that they stock it with sufficient animals to justify their claim. Current rate is a halfpenny a year for each sheep, a penny-halfpenny a head cows and around three pence for each horse. Oh, and then there is a ten-pound licence fee annually.”

“All cash that has to be collected by the government. Good luck to them finding some of these folk out here.”

“I have agreed to send back, as far as can be accounted for, regular statements of squatters I encounter, and their stock,” Tim said.

“And good luck to you lad. I don’t think any of us has taken into account how vast this country is. I think we have barely explored half of it as yet. Who knows what lies in the very centre? I’ve heard tales of a vast inland sea. Perhaps Billy’s people will let us know, if he ever finds them.”

They rode in companionable silence for a while. The plodding of the oxen, the murmurs from their handler and his mates, added to the heat, began to lull Tim into a kind of lassitude. When he spotted a small group of natives possibly a half mile away, outlined against the afternoon sun, he said, “Those people and their ancestors have survived on this land forever it seems, yet they have no need of licences or fees for their animals. They roam free and live off the fruits of the land."

Carlos grunted. "Oh, aye and has that not upset more than a few of the settlers!"

Tim swore beneath his breath. "Settlers who should learn to live alongside them, and perhaps learn from them instead of slaughtering the poor souls who dare to set foot on land they have trod all their lives in peace."

Carlos pointed a finger towards Billy, now riding alongside Jo just behind Jacko's wagon. "Have you learnt how that young native happens to be travelling with the girl? Seems an odd companion for a wench. Don't say a lot, does he? Is he mute?"

"By all accounts the lad was working with her parents out at the mine. He went back to town with her I guess rather than stay out in the mountains alone. And no, he is no mute, just keeps to himself." Tim went on to explain about the horrific killing of her parents and the other miners.

"My God, poor wench. Why would she choose to drag herself overland with you, I wonder?"

"Wonder no more, dear uncle. She is in search of excitement and adventure I believe. I assured you she was no ordinary wench did I not? And she is not chasing me, more a life of her own I guess."

Carlos rubbed his chin thoughtfully. "Hmm, do not be so sure. I have lived longer than you lad, and most women do things because they have a plan in mind, a plan that often includes some poor hapless male. Mark my words, she sees you as a likely candidate for marriage." He chuckled.

Tim made a small scoffing noise. "You are barking up the wrong tree there, my man. I doubt the thought of a husband has even entered her head." On saying that, Tim recollected she had mentioned that very thing when they were discussing this journey south. But no, that was merely some frivolous joke, meaning nothing. He quickly pushed that aside, saying, "She is not some silly little chit as I first thought but a woman of means who will be able to take her pick of the nobs once we reach our destination. And Billy is off in search of his people—the people he was taken from as a child."

"A woman of means, you say? Hmm, I might even toss my hat her way. She is a comely lass I'll give her that, and plucky. Not many women would dare to do what she has decided to do, unless they were accompanying their husbands."

Tim swore. "Do not even think so Carlos. You are an old man and she is still a virtuous young woman despite her appearance. Keep your thoughts of lechery and whatever else away from her."

"I am insulted. Old man indeed? I am barely past my thirty-sixth year and in my prime." He chuckled to soften his outburst. "Mark my words an older man with experience is what she needs. And I am not even a decade her senior. Tiger is eleven years older than your Mama, and they seem to be making the best of life."

Tim made no comment on that. It was true that many women, especially new settlers arriving from the old country, sought out the older men in the community, perhaps surmising they would be wealthier—or perhaps expecting them to die soon and leave their gained wealth to their young wife. Also true, was that when his father and mother first met, his Mama was not yet twenty. Admittedly, they did not wed for a few more years, but that was because of circumstances, or so Papa often said. He never went into the circumstances that kept them apart too deeply, but Tim did know his Mama had always been a stubborn woman—a trait Tim was aware had caused much friction in the early days, especially during the journey across the mountains.

He sighed inwardly. Perhaps women were stronger than men. They might appear weak and perhaps were unable to lift heavy weights but when he looked around at those close to him, it was true that most women made up their minds well before the man had even had time to dwell on their intentions. He wasn't sure if the idea of Jo setting her sights on becoming his wife pleased or worried him, so he decided it was likely Carlos was simply jesting with him, and pushed it out of his mind. There were many other things to worry about right now.

"I am pausing for a moment," he called, and Jacko waved over his shoulder to let Tim know he had heard but did not falter.

"Do not get too far behind," he shouted, as Tim dismounted. He took down his water bag, and after taking a swig poured some into his hat, which he offered to Bracken, who drank his fill. "Good boy."

Intent on his dog he had not noticed that Jo had also dismounted, until she asked, "Will he be walking all the way to Port Philip?"

"No, that is why I stopped. I wanted to see how his paws were faring. He is a strong animal, used to running alongside me over many miles, but I feel he has walked enough for today." His paws seemed to be in good order, but the last thing Tim wanted was for his dog to become lame.

"Why not let him ride atop the pack horse," she suggested.

Tim ruffled his hair before replacing his hat "That idea occurred to me. We will try. If it does not prove successful, then I will ask Jacko if he can spend part of each day on the wagon. It depends on how stony the trail is once the road becomes less defined. Come lad," he said as he bent to pull Bracken into his arms.

The hound willingly allowed Tim to hoist him onto the back of the pack. The horses they had selected were sturdy and the animal would have no trouble carrying the extra weight of his dog. Bracken settled down quite comfortably amid the load. "Good lad." Tim patted him on the head before remounting.

The wagon and riders were well ahead so they picked up their pace and soon caught up. "How are you faring?" he asked. Jo certainly seemed no worse for wear, in fact still looked as fresh as she did at early morn.

She grinned. Tim was certain she looked on this as a grand lark. "I am faring well, kind sire," she said.

“Tell me, what plans do you have for yourself once we reach Port Philip?” If we do reach that far—he added to himself. It was estimated that it would take them nigh on a month to reach the south coastline and Port Philip, and day one was not at an end yet. It was as Carlos said, this land was vast, and they had a long journey ahead. Perhaps he was foolhardy to contemplate it, but they had come too far to turn back, and he had dreamed of doing such for a very long time.

She wrinkled her nose as if in thought. “Do you know, I have not given that a lot of thought. I was intent on seeking adventure, and you offered it—albeit unwittingly.”

“Of that you can be certain. I still cannot believe you planned this all along without murmuring a word of your intentions.”

“Huh, if I so much as said one word of my intentions you would have doubtlessly ensured I did no such thing and would probably have made certain your Aunt Sara had me confined in some way. You cannot seem to understand that I am a determined person.” She sighed. “I think perhaps I have a smidgen of my Pa’s stubbornness within me and will always seek adventure as against the easy and simple life.”

“Stubborn is so right. You are the most single-minded female I have ever come across. I sincerely hope you do not live to regret it.” Tim rubbed his jaw.

He caught sight of her nibbling her lower lip. Was she uncertain, despite her act of bravado? “I am sure I will not. Tell, me Timothy, are you so terribly mad at me for doing this?”

He had to think about that. After his initial shock wore off, he did have to concede that it would certainly liven the journey up to have this unusual wench along. But he was not about to tell her that. “Honestly Jo, I am still trying to decide on that. There will be so many drawbacks to having a female along. Some of them I have already pointed out. If you had been included in our plans—just supposing I had agreed to it, we would have ensured you had a wagon or cart so at certain times you could be assured of privacy.”

She waved that idea aside with a soft word of derision. "Forget I am a female. Despite the fact that you journeyed across the mountains with your mother as a child and have since made countless crossings since to see your kin, you still have a strange notion that women are feeble and need coddling. You should never forget that your own mama was a convict as was mine, but they were strong women who overcame adversity, did they not?" With another small sound she added, "You will see that I am not a silly wench who needs fussing over."

Tim sincerely hoped not. And, he found the idea of forgetting her a female was so out of the question it was ridiculous. Despite her manly outfit, no one could ever think of her as a man once they got to know her.

"Do you know nothing of the women who have helped New South Wales become the prosperous settlement it is?" she asked.

"I have to say I am guilty, but no, I have had little cause to look outside my family for female inspiration. I have a feeling that Annie might prove a handful for some poor unsuspecting male one day." He chuckled.

"You are correct, your sister and I share many opinions. That is one reason we became friends. She was as irked as I when voting was introduced just recently, and it appears that we females are never to be given such rights." Her small sound of disgust expressed her opinion of that.

"I have no doubt that women such as yourself and Annie will not be shy of telling men what you think of such a decision. So tell me, who are these other women who have performed such miraculous changes?" Tim asked the question not so much out of curiosity, but more because he liked her enthusiasm, and hoped it never dwindled. Life was still hard enough in the colony for most men, let alone for their womenfolk, who often became overloaded with the daily grind of the difficulties of life here. His mother complained at times that although she was a lot better off than some of her contemporaries, there were still many things that could be improved on. Perhaps it would be women such as his dear sisters, and this wench here, who would make such improvements.

"You must know of Governor Macquarie's wife, Elizabeth. She supported her husband loyally through all his tumultuous years. As you must recall he had very forthright opinions on emancipists, which earned him many enemies. She willingly accompanied her husband to Van Diemen's Land, a treacherous voyage, and she went with him on his journey across the Mountains to Bathurst. After her death five years ago, the grand lady was granted two thousand acres of land for her descendants. And you must know that she, along with Elizabeth Macarthur, were the first to suggest the idea of producing hay as fodder for the animals."

"Yes, as a matter of fact I did know all this." However, if he was to be honest, it obviously meant more to this female than to him. Perhaps having a strong-willed mother, he had merely considered most women possessed such abilities. Some just chose to live dull but peaceful lives where they obeyed their husband's every demand.

"And did you know of Elizabeth Macarthur? Now there is another woman of substance." She looked off into the distance, perhaps dreaming of the changes she herself was going to make. "Her husband had controversy surrounding him due to his part in the rebellion against Governor Bligh, which must have made her position awkward, but never seemed to faze her. He built Elizabeth Farm for her out at Parramatta. When he left the colony to return to England, it was Elizabeth who managed the large merino flocks. For eight years in his absence she ventured into dangerous territory overseeing their flocks, all this while violence went on between the settlers and natives."

"And is this what you would like to do when we reach our destination?" Tim asked. How was it that he had known this female for a year without an inkling of how knowledgeable she was? "Own land and become a sheep farmer?"

With a small shrug, she said, "I will wait and see. My teacher, Matilda, reinforced Mama's wish that instead of following a man and bowing down to his wishes as Mama had done, I must follow my own dreams."

"And these dreams are?"

"I should like to be remembered for my deeds. A woman has come into the news only recently. Caroline Chisholm, although born in England, arrived here two years ago from Madras with her much older husband. In Madras, she founded a school for daughters of European soldiers, so it was probably not chance that when her husband, a Captain, was recalled to service last year, she began to meet every migrant ship that arrived, knowing the females on board would be requiring work here in the colony. She housed some of these women in her home until finding suitable employment for them. At the start of this year, she approached the Governor and Lady Gipps with a proposition of starting a home for her female immigrants. Her plan is to settle these women in employment in the outer areas where landowners find it difficult to find workers."

"Yes, I did hear of her work. It was publicised in the Sydney Herald newspaper. She was granted use of part of the old immigration barracks. I agree, she is a remarkable woman, as are the others you mentioned. And you plan to do similar work once we reach Port Philip?"

"Hmm, as I said, I will wait until we reach our destination before I decide. And perhaps fate will decide which path I will take." She turned to face him, a wide grin on her face—a face that was rather grubby by now, as his likely was. "And now you must tell me your dreams. I have little idea of your intentions once we reach the end of this momentous journey."

"Short of sending back regular reports to the Government offices on the situation down south and the hazards we encounter I am, like you, without true intentions. So we will take what fate offers us, shall we?"

She laughed merrily at that. The woman did not seem to tire. They said little as the afternoon wore on. The sun was getting low on the horizon when they spotted a jumble of buildings in the distance.

“We will spend the night here,” Jacko shouted as he gestured ahead. “Do not expect a hostelry. I would suggest you use your tents rather than stay in his flea-ridden hovel. But you can get a good solid feed if you so require, he runs a good kitchen with fresh-killed mutton to satisfy our hunger.”

* * *

Tim wasn’t quite sure what annoyed him more, that his dog had forsaken him for the company of Jo, and lay close at her side, or that Jo chatted away merrily with one of Jacko’s helpers, a man not much older than he. They had all eaten a filling meal as Jacko forecast, at what passed as an inn, but was merely a shed with various outhouses attached to it. Then, instead of going to the tent that Billy set up for her, as Tim expected, she sauntered across to where the bullock driver and his men were sitting around their fire, most puffing away on their pipes.

The native lad sat alone, his back against a solid eucalyptus, so Tim went to his side. Along the way, the boy had barely spoken more than a few words. What words he did utter could not be criticized, for he sounded as if he too had shared in Jo’s lessons and was as well spoken as some men Tim knew who had attended King’s School alongside him. “Tell me, Billy…” Tim said as he sat beside him. “Do you have a notion of where you might find members of your lost kinsfolk?”

Billy shook his dark head. His hair was as black as the night sky and as curly as a sheep fleece. “No sir, I was told my people came from down south.” He rubbed his chin as he shrugged. “A lot of my kind have been killed, so perhaps I may never find my close kin.”

“That’s sad.” Tim meant that sincerely. He could not comprehend a life without knowing his family, or where he came from. They sat in quiet contemplation. Jo rose, glanced about, and seeing him sitting alongside Billy, sauntered over to stand above them. Bracken wagged his tail and licked Tim’s hand.

"I would have thought you would be in haste to get to your tent after such a strenuous day," Tim said. "Instead of dallying with the men." He knew he sounded like a strict father, but she seemed amused and laughed, which annoyed him more.

"I was hardly dallying, merely having a conversation with a man who seems polite and interested. It is a beautiful night do you not think?"

"Of course he's interested in you—you are the sole female among a group of hardened men and should be more careful."

"Careful?" She made a small sound of disdain.

"Yes, careful. Your familiarity could be taken the wrong way. You are well aware of what I am suggesting Madam, so don't play the innocent."

"Innocent? Am I not allowed to pass a few moments in sensible conversation with someone near my own age?" She turned to walk away, and Bracken trailed her.

Tim jumped to his feet and followed her. He caught her by the arm. "And kindly stop repeating my words. You are obviously used to rough men, I agree, and because of your upbringing have not yet learned the ways of some men, I imagine."

"Don't you dare criticise my upbringing. My parents were wise and taught me well. I know how to behave in polite society, despite what you might think of me. Did I not behave as a respectable woman while visiting in your Uncles' home? Had I not told you of the incident that forced me to come back to town, you would not have an inkling of how I spent my early years." She glared at him. "And do not presume that because I tagged along with you on this journey that you have the right to give me orders. I thought I had made it plain that I am an independent woman who knows her own mind. I certainly do not need you to tell me how to behave and who to talk to."

Thankfully, they were a short distance away from the others, for her voice had risen. "You made the decision to join us, tagging along as you so rightly put it, without my permission I might add, but this does not give you the right to expect to dally with the first man along the way who shows you attention, do you hear me?" Tim wanted to shake her but satisfied himself with clutching her arm.

"Don't you dare think to dictate to me what I should or should not do." She shook him off and stalked away.

"I have every right to dictate to you, Madam. Just because you have rigged yourself out in men's clothing and ride like a man, the fact is that you are a female and there are men who would take this as being…" he ran out of steam and words to explain how he felt.

"Being what? A whore?" She shook a finger at him. "You are insulting and rude, sir."

"Rude I may be, but who is to tell you if I do not? At times, you act like a spoiled child, Jo, and at others make it clear that you are a woman who knows her own mind. On a journey such as this, you would be wise to listen to me. Who else would you turn to if you need assistance?"

"I do not need your assistance or anyone else's, do you hear me? If you had taken my offer of becoming my husband as I proposed, then you might have been in a position to tell me what to do and who I should talk to. You refused, so therefore forsook any rights you might have had."

Tim was so mad then he could easily have spanked her hide. "You are ridiculous. Your suggestion of marriage was merely a nonsense idea and no more a serious proposal than…" He ran out of words again. Why did this woman make him act at times as if he had no more sense than a lad of tender years? "…than the words of a spoilt brat who wanted to get her own way." Once those words came out, he knew exactly how stupid they were. This woman had never been spoilt or pampered in her life.

"I am ridiculous? Do you hear yourself?" she spat. "I will now take myself off to my tent." With that, she stalked off, head held high. Bracken looked from her to Tim, his black face bearing a look that could only be read as confused.

"Go with her, boy, and keep an eye on her." Tim waved a hand and Bracken bounded after her.

Billy was now secure in his swag beneath the tree, sleeping soundly. Tim wondered what he thought of his mistress and her behaviour. No doubt, he would keep his thoughts to himself as always.

Not so Carlos. His uncle strode towards him, grinning. "You let the chit get the best of you, boy," he said with a chuckle.

"Do you suggest I let the wench dally with the men? Lord knows what mischief she will get up to, and this is just day one of our journey." Tim sighed.

"As long as we keep an eye on her, it would likely be best for your peace of mind if you do not try to change her."

"You are suddenly an expert on the behaviour of females, are you?" Now Tim was getting annoyed with his uncle, and it was all her fault. "Why do you believe she decided to tag along with us—and do not give me the stupid reasons you came up with about her setting her sights on me. She proved once and for all this night that she thinks I am nothing but a domineering male who wishes to rule over her and disregard her wishes. Lord above knows what pickle I would be in if I had gone along with her stupid suggestion and married the confounded chit."

"Perhaps that would have been the wisest decision." Carlos roared with laughter before walking off to relieve himself behind a bush. When he joined Tim in their tent, he was still chuckling.

"Heaven help any poor male who gets caught up in that woman's tomfooleries," Tim muttered before rolling over and yawning.

Chapter Four

The sun was warm, even as it barely rose above the horizon. The destination this day was Liverpool. According to Jacko, the town was thriving, and he reckoned it would be an ideal place for them to stop, as they would be assured of decent accommodation. Tim had a feeling it might perhaps be the last place they would be able to get such for many miles. Small towns were cropping up along their route, but none as advanced as Liverpool. Jacko's soft chuckle as he mentioned this made Tim suspicious.

Jo and he barely exchanged more than a few abrupt words while preparing for the day ahead, and she now rode alongside the man she had been so freely chatting with last evening. Tim was certain she did this in her determination to annoy him more. To add to his annoyance one of Jacko's other sidekicks had eyed Jo with a look that could only mean he had intentions that were not honourable.

He heaved a sigh. Let her get herself into a pickle—he had done his part in warning her of her foolishness with being free and easy, and washed his hands of her. Having made that decision, he then realised how stupid that was. The chit may not have been invited along on this journey, but nonetheless he felt responsible for her, like it or not. Heaven help him if it got back to his Aunt Sara—or Mama—if he did not protect her as a gentleman was bound to.

As he rode, it came to Tim that he had little idea about women, their real needs and desires. Perhaps Jo was a typical female, and his judgement in thinking her unusual was wrong. His sister Annie was just sixteen, Rose a year younger and his other sister, Mary, still a child at eleven or so, so to him they were all merely children. The thought that before long they would be adults causing mayhem now caused him unrest.

His meagre experiences to date with females other than family had taught him naught when he thought about it. “At the risk of intruding on matters of a personal nature, might I ask you a question?” Tim turned to ask Carlos who rode alongside him.

Carlos looked askance at that. “Tim, my lad, ask away. You know I am always here for you and will help if I can.”

“You have doubtless had many females swooning after you. It is no secret that Uncle Remy’s dark looks and hair are something that women seem to find attractive, and you share such an appearance. What have you learned along the way of women and their wiles?”

Carlos’ burst of laughter rang out and gained the attention of Jo as well as the man riding alongside her. “Tim, my boy, if I live to be one hundred years or more, I will never learn what goes on inside their pretty little heads.” He tapped his mop of burnished hair. “They are a mystery to me and to most men.” With a finger to his brow, he added, “Half the fun is trying to find out what their intentions are.”

“Have you been truly swept away by any one female in particular? There must have been a few out at Bathurst who eyed you with interest?”

Carlos pulled a wry face. “The aim is to always be on guard. I had a married woman who set her sights on me, but when I learned that her husband was in the military, I kept my distance. Military men are handy with their rifles, and I fancy keeping my head. I have been in love.” He looked pensive as he admitted this.

“Really? Tell me, will you? Why are you not back there in Bathurst settled down to a life of marital bliss with your love?”

Carlos sighed. “Alas, my story is similar to that of my brother Remy, her father was too rich and high and mighty to consider an ex-con as a fitting partner for his daughter. Unlike Remy, who had the similar problem when he first met sweet Sara, I realised I would not win her hand, ever.

To be honest, Tim, I fled, and that is how I ended up here with you."

"But did you not think it worth the fight to win her?"

"Alas, no." He shrugged. "Some battles are not worth the effort. But I think I have not answered your question, have I? What you really wish to know is how to choose between love and lust, is it not?"

Tim rubbed his chin. "I wasn't really sure what I was asking, Carlos. I realise that my knowledge of women in every sense of the word is slight. I have visited a brothel or two but find that repugnant if I am honest. Am I foolish to wish for something other than gaining satisfaction with a well-used strumpet? I know many men, even long-married men, are satisfied with their mistresses, but am I a fool for wanting more?"

"Tim, my lad, you are a true romantic. Take my advice, scant as it is, and wait until you find a maiden who cares enough about you that she is willing to forego everything for you."

"But how will I know if she is such a one?"

"Oh, you will know, believe me. I will tell you now in all honesty, the reason I fled and did not pursue my chosen love was because she was not willing to forsake her life of wealth and pampering to chance a life with a poor sheep farm worker such as myself."

"That is a sorry tale, Carlos. But cheer up, when we reach our final destination there will be many available fair maidens and you will surely find another such love."

"As you yourself will, Tim my boy." He gestured towards the wench still in conversation with the bullock driver's helper. "Do not forsake the idea that the little miss there has not set her cap at you. You could do a lot worse. She has spirit, I'll give her that." With a grin, he tipped his hat forward.

"She now despises me, I am certain. I feel she is too impulsive, else why would she even consider following us. And then, the little minx has the audacity to claim I have no right to give her my opinion. Does she not see that I am merely looking out for her welfare?" He gestured toward the older man who had been eyeing her lasciviously. “Her free and easy manner has attracted the attention of that fellow named Archie, I notice.”

“Hmm, I too took heed of that. I will give him a warning when we reach Liverpool. Meanwhile it looks as if we are stopping.” While they had been in conversation, the clouds had moved in, and now covered the sun.

Jacko looked to the sky and shouted. “We will rest here. It looks like rain, so we’ll put the billy on for tea.”

* * *

It began to rain, not heavily, but steadily, as they moved off after a brief break. A short time later, they saw a mob of sheep ahead. Jacko called out to the three drovers, and they hailed him, before herding the sheep to the side of the road. “Where you headed?” Jacko shouted as his wagon drew level with them.

“South, until we find land that suits us,” one of the squatters said, as he gestured to his flock. “They’re fine beasts, and we shall find pastures that suit.”

“Good luck to you and keep an eye out for the natives. They don’t take kindly to white men crossing land they see as theirs.”

The driver sneered and raised a fist. “They best not interfere with us. This is our land—the governor said so.”

Tim cursed beneath his breath. The proclamation by Governor Bourke five years ago, claiming that no one owned this land before the British decided to settle here, had irked him then and did so still. “These men are rough types, the sort who will attack the natives without asking questions,” he muttered. One of the spurs that started him thinking of heading south had been the overland trek taken by Hawdon, Gardiner and Hepburn. Just four years ago, the men had successfully driven three hundred cattle to Port Phillip, so ensuring many would wish to follow their example.

It was unfortunate that some of the types who chose to follow in their trail were uncouth men doing it for personal gain alone. Many of the squatters were learning that it took more than a flock of sheep and a desire to make money. Some had already fallen on hard times, so he had heard, unable to pay the government licences. Shepherds often were left to guard large flocks, which proved difficult in hilly country where the sheep were easy prey for hungry roving dingoes, the native dog.

Only last year the price of wool had fallen, making conditions worse for some. It was likely that this flock would end up sent to the boiling vats to make tallow. A trade had built up since the demand for more soap and candles in the colony. The process sickened Tim when he had been sent to where the sheep were herded to be slaughtered, skinned and boiled.

The man who had been talking was now looking at Billy, who happened to be at the rear alongside Jo. He lifted his filthy hat and waved it towards the native lad. "What 'ya doing with one of them in your party, man?" he asked roughly. "Is he yer dogsbody? That's all they are fit for."

Jo wore a protective cape that she'd donned when the rain began, the hood pulled well down to cover the top half of her face. Tim cursed inwardly when she pushed it back and shouted, "He is with me. And keep your opinions to yourself, you scum!"

"Well, well, if it ain't a female. And one with a black fella to keep her warm at night." The man moved closer and Tim angled his horse alongside Jo's. Bracken's hackles were raised, and he growled low in his throat.

Tim murmured reassurance at the dog as he glared at Jo. Why did she have to open her pretty little mouth? "The woman is right, man. What the native is doing along with us is of no concern of yours. Now take yourself off and tend your flock. And you would be wise in future to do as the lady says, and not be so free with your opinions."

The man looked shocked for a moment, and slowly dismounted, a fist at the ready. Bracken's growl grew deeper. "Back off boy," Tim said softly, as he too dismounted, and his dog obeyed, still growling low.

Jacko had been watching with interest, but once the man had both feet on the ground, he left his place on his wagon and rushed across to put himself between Tim and the fellow. "We don't want trouble. Take the advice offered and be on your way. Your sheep are in need of rounding up, I fear. You best get yourself some decent drovers if you aim to make this your living."

Jacko was right. The sheep had begun to graze and a few of them were some distance away from the main flock already, the two drovers trying to herd them back. The man swore viciously, quickly scrambled back onto his horse and shouted over a shoulder as he rode off, "You better not come across me again on your travels, me boys."

Turning to Jo Tim said, "Let that be a lesson, Madam. You would do best to keep to your own advice and be careful what you say in future. As you have informed me on numerous occasions, you have been used to living among rough types, but there is a time for speaking your mind and a time for playing dumb. I hope to goodness we do not come across him again."

She did not respond, but her mouth was held in a stiff line that indicated she was finding it very difficult not to have her say.

Tim lifted Bracken atop the packhorse, patted him as he settled down comfortably, and they moved off. No one spoke for some time. The rain stopped and the sun appeared, making it steamy and uncomfortable, so they all removed their wet weather protection.

When Tim grew tired of the wench's silence, he decided to see if he could raise her ire again. It was more fun when she was arguing with him. During the long stretches of silence and the tedium of the long ride, he had come to the conclusion that she was wayward and unlikely to heed any advice he gave her, so he would do best to try to ignore it.

Drawing alongside her horse, he asked, "You have forsaken your new friend?"

"Contrary to what you think of me, I do listen at times to you when your advice is sound," she said with a small twist to her mouth as if it was distasteful for her to admit such. "Much as I enjoyed conversation with another of similar age and temperament as myself, I did notice that the other two fellows accompanying Jacko were giving me looks I found distasteful." She shrugged. "Don't become smug—I would have realised my error even if you had not warned me that I was behaving in a manner not befitting a lady." The last word was delivered with a touch of scorn.

"Good to hear. 'Tis a strange situation we find ourselves in, Josephine." She gave her head a little shake at his use of her full name. "I am at a loss how to behave with you. I would never wish to come across as a hard headed father figure, but let us face it, you have put me in this position. You cannot depend on Billy for protection either. He has many of his own obstacles to cross, as you saw with that cur of a fellow."

"I do beg your pardon." That was said with such sarcasm he almost laughed.

Tim sighed. The wench was incorrigible. "Did you think this through carefully before you made the momentous decision to join us on our travels? Did you confide in anyone at all or ask advice?"

She didn't answer for a while, and Tim began to wonder if perhaps she had no answer to give. Headstrong as she was, it was doubtful if she even considered how she would manage amongst a group of men on such a difficult ride.

"I listened in on your plans with your uncle, as you may recall. And, do you forget I mentioned more than once that I wished to travel. Oh, and I did a lot of reading," she said.

"You did, did you?" Now that she mentioned it, Tim recalled that she seemed to be loitering somewhere nearby while he and Carlos were discussing plans with Uncle Remy. At that time, he surmised that her mention of travelling was simply whimsy. Not many women in the colony chose to travel of their own free will—it was usually the wish of their husbands or in the case of a servant, their master. "Please tell me what this reading consisted of?"

"Well, I have spent a lot of time at the library in my leisure hours. I do love books, don't you?" Without waiting for his answer, she continued, "I read the newspapers too, believe it or not. Would you like me to quote some facts I learned?"

"Please do." Tim waved a hand.

"I know that the road south to Liverpool was begun in 1814, and that the bridges along the way were designed and built by David Lennox. It was governor Macquarie who encouraged settlement to the south of the colony and therefore the first plans for the road were put into action."

The chit certainly knew a lot more than most of the other females of her age that he had met. "But you do realise that the further south we travel, the road becomes more inhospitable. We have seen the best of it to now."

"Yes, I read the article in the Herald newspaper early this year written by Timothy Bushman in which he states that the road is uninteresting, and the view consists mainly of gum trees and public houses. He stated that once the traveler passes Yass, there is no accommodation on offer and so therefore we will be fending for ourselves." She looked across at him. "I suppose you think me odd to give up a life of ease to chase what many may see as a foolish, girlish wish for adventure."

When he thought about it, her wish for adventure differed little from his own. Uncle Remy and Aunt Sara were of the same opinion as Mama and Papa. He had good employment and a comfortable life in Sydney. Why forsake it and all the pleasures to be had to go off in search of something new? It wasn't as if he was a sheep farmer in search of fresh green pastures. He had no set plan in mind of what he would do once he reached Port Philip, only a desire to seek excitement, much as she did.

"No, I do not see you as foolish to seek adventure. What I do consider foolish is that you did not consult me or ask my permission to ride along with us." He could tell by her expression that she did not like that word. Perhaps permission was too strong to use, but nonetheless she had put him in a position where he felt obliged to keep an eye out for her. Who knew what trouble she would provoke next?

"Perhaps I should stop over in Liverpool and seek a party travelling back to Sydney," she suggested.

For all his annoyance at her for being foolhardy and making rash decisions, did he really want rid of her? Deep down, Tim knew that she had livened what was really a tedious journey with her wit and at times childish behaviour. Despite this behaviour, she showed a rare intelligence. She also shared his deep interest in the wildlife.

As that thought crossed his mind, she said softly, "Oh look, the kangaroos have young along with them."

A mob were a short distance away and as they made to take off at seeing the intruders, a couple of joeys quickly jumped into the protection of their mother's pouch. It always amazed Tim how fast they could hop using their huge tails to balance.

"Billy told me that he thinks his people might have come from around this area. The Darugs, as he called them, were probably driven off by the early settlers in these parts." She curled her lip. "They were harmless folk, used to living off the land—land that was taken from them by force and bloodshed."

Billy must have heard what she said for he nodded in her direction as if in acknowledgement of her words. "Perhaps he could seek out information about this tribe when we reach Liverpool," Tim said.

"I would hate to part with him, but everyone belongs with their own kind." She sat quietly for a while, and then said, "When Governor Macquarie left the colony, it is said he remarked after he first visited this area that the land around Liverpool was densely forested. No doubt, these forests have largely disappeared since the white settlers decided to do as they like with land that had always been cared for by the native tribes. People who cared not for fancy houses and lived in basic huts that could be moved as they wandered at will."

"It is also fact that their tribal system and set of rituals are far superior to us white folk."

She nodded, and they rode in a kind of companionable silence as the road took them closer to Liverpool. Now and then, they could see a small dwelling off in the distance, likely a shepherd's hut where he slept at night, after herding his flock into a makeshift pen to protect them from prowling dingoes. Most shepherds had reliable dogs who were an asset in remote areas such as this.

Tim remembered his Pa's old work-roughened shepherd Mole, who had worked for Tiger for as far back as Tim could recall. So accustomed to his lonely life, he could never be encouraged to sleep in the house, and was often heard muttering to himself, or to his faithful dogs as he went about his duties.

"We reach Liverpool within the hour," Jacko shouted, surprising Tim out of a kind of lethargy, brought on by the sun and the monotony. "We will stop at the cattle yards to unload our wares, and you will find safe yards there for your animals before you find suitable accommodation in town."

Tim had learned that Jacko was a man of few words, and that was likely the only advice he would give them.

"Billy will stay with the animals," Jo said. "He will take good care of them, do not fear."

Tim was relieved at that, as he had been worrying about the boy's reception if he turned up at a rooming house or hotel with them. It might have proved embarrassing for him as well as them.

True to Jacko's word, they were soon crossing the grand bridge that David Lennox designed, which was built only a few years ago by convicts. Liverpool was indeed a growing town, with several government buildings that Tim knew of. The governor had been especially proud of the newly opened wharf in the centre of town, where vessels that traded with Sydney could easily unload and load their cargoes.

The cattle yards were as they were anywhere, noisy and riotous, with a mass of people, animals and smells. With Jacko's help, they soon found stabling for their horses and Tim felt at ease leaving Billy to ensure they received fodder and shelter overnight. "Where will you sleep, Billy?" he asked.

The lad nodded. "Where else but with the horses. I am happy to share their bed with them."

For a minimal fee, Tim ensured that their packs were stowed safely away and not left where any passing rogue could take a fancy to them. He also made sure that Billy was assured of a good meal. Jacko and his three helpers would be sleeping with their wagon. "Have no fear, I'll keep me eye on the lad," Jacko said before they left the yards.

Carrying all they would need to see them overnight, Tim, Carlos and Jo headed for the nearest boarding house where they had been told they could get a meal and a clean bed. "The governor had every right to be proud of this town," Tim said as they passed near the brick-built hospital. "If you have need of anything, there is also a store, Jo. You would do well to get any provisions you require here."

All the womenfolk he knew took great pleasure in visiting Sara's emporium, or any store for that matter where all sorts of fripperies that women required were stocked. This wench likely had come along well prepared. She proved that by saying, "I have no need of anything at this time, thank you."

When they entered what passed for a hotel, a short man with a huge whiskery face beamed at them as he said, "Welcome gents, room with three beds, is it?"

Tim hid a smile when he saw a look of embarrassment cross Jo's face. "No, that will be one room for this lady here." He gestured her way, and caught the grin that Carlos failed to hide. "And another with two beds. And can we order a meal, sir?"

The man looked taken aback and stared at Jo as if he thought Tim lied. "As you wish. Two rooms it is. Do you wish them side by side?"

"Yes, that will do nicely. You have no objection to my dog do you? He is well mannered."

He glanced down at Bracken who wagged his tail as if to prove he was friendly. "No, that will be no problem, sir. Top of the stairs. First two doors on the left, both facing the street. Does the…lady…" He made a harrumphing noise in his throat, before adding, "Need warm water for bathing?"

"Yes, that would be lovely," Jo said demurely.

Still looking confused, he said, "Right, I'll send a maid up right away. Just make yourself comfy. That'll be one pound and ten shillings each, including the meal, thank you sir." He nodded at Tim. "And the dining room is along the passage there. Any time that suits, the kitchen is open for service. Oh, and the privy is outside the back door. We have not caught up with the big hotel yet, with their inside lavatories and even a room for bathing."

Carlos and Tim thanked him, and they went up the stairs. Tim opened the first door on the landing. "This one will be yours, Madam." He waved a hand and bowed slightly.

"I will repay you what I owe," Jo said as she entered the small space. A bed suitable for a child, and a small dresser holding a washbasin were the bare furnishings.

"No need." Tim went across to the small window that did indeed overlook the street below. "Call if you need anything," he added as a tiny girl carrying a jug of water she could barely tote entered.

"I will be fine." Jo tossed her hat on the bed and turned to the girl, saying, "Thank you, that will be all for now."

"Let us know when you are refreshed, and we will go down for a meal. I must admit I am hungry," Tim said as he and Carlos went out.

Carlos sat on one of the beds and he and Tim stared at each other. "Well, that was amusing," Carlos commented. "Perhaps the wench now sees her mistake. I vouch we will meet up with such in other places along the way. To be honest, Tim, I am at a loss to understand why her ma and pa allowed her such freedom. There must have been men at the mines who had foul intentions. Surely she hasn't come this far in life without being harassed."

Tim sighed. "She no doubt thought that cutting off her locks and donning men's clothing would suffice."

"Her slenderness goes some way to helping with her disguise, but it only takes a second glance to see that beneath the rough shirt there is a…" Carlos waved his hands about in front of him. "…a comely female's body."

With a shrug, Tim decided not to answer. She most definitely had an admirable female body, but he was not about to let Carlos know that he had noticed. He turned his back, and after pouring water from a jug into the washbowl, washed his hands and splashed water on his face. "I will grow a beard," he decided, and Carlos agreed that he might do likewise.

In no time, Jo was knocking at the door. Tim noticed she had donned a clean shirt. Without the hat there was no mistaking that she was female. Perhaps it never occurred to her that her disguise would have fared better if she thought to bind her breasts. He was not about to tell her.

The dining room held three tables and two elderly men sat at one of them deep in conversation, ignoring their presence. The same girl who brought the water came and asked if they would like to order their dinner. There was little choice, as it seemed the menu consisted of roast lamb and vegetables. "Could I also have meat for my dog?" Tim asked, and she nodded, before scampering back to the kitchen.

The meal was delicious, and they sent their compliments to the cook. When they got up to leave, the long clock against the wall said it was nine-thirty. Jo wished to use the privy, so Tim and Carlos loitered nearby in the small but pleasant garden behind the house. A raucous din spoilt the tranquility of the warm evening. "I feel we have chosen unwisely," Tim said.

Carlos agreed. "I did notice that the public house was across the street. I thought I might take myself over there—

for just one ale or two to quench my thirst. What do you say?"

"You go ahead, I am weary and will stay here." He nodded towards Jo who was now filling a bucket for Bracken at the water pump. She then held her hands beneath, drying them down the sides of her trousers. "I will ensure the wench is safely in her bed."

"Fair enough." Carlos waved and headed down a small pathway at the side of the house, whistling softly as he walked.

Tim opened the door and ushered Jo inside. The passageway was dim. She stumbled and Tim reached to catch her by the arm. They said nothing as they continued up the stairs. He opened the door to her room and when she went inside, he had a sudden urge to talk awhile. "Do you wish to sleep?" he asked, not knowing what else to say, feeling suddenly almost shy, which was ridiculous. This was Josephine, and the pair of them had spent many occasions together in the past. There was something very intimate about this small room with the bed occupying most of the space.

"I think I will sketch for a while. I need to get impressions of the day down on my page. And perhaps I might not get the use of a lamp elsewhere." She upped the flame in the lamp as she spoke and shadows danced on the walls, making the room seem even more intimate.

That was a surprise. Before this journey, Tim had no idea she could draw. She pulled out a scroll from her pack and sitting on the side of the bed unrolled it before her. "May I see?" he asked.

With a small nod, she gestured to her side. Tim knelt on the floor to get a better look. She had already drawn numerous birds of many colours, and animals, including kangaroos with their young, a sugar glider, and an echidna, amongst others. All delicately coloured and so lifelike Tim was amazed.

"You have a rare talent, Jo. How is it I didn't know you were an artist?"

She laughed. "It is usually something I do when alone. What did you think I did on my long rides out of town? There are so many wonderful creatures in this world, why would I not wish to get them down for others to see at some time in the future?"

"But where did you learn? Who taught you? Someone must have given you direction. We all like to scribble as children, even I imagined I could draw at one stage—but my childish sketching would never compare to yours." Tim pointed to a cockatoo with its crest of yellow feathers.

"Matilda was gifted. I feel she would have been a great artist had not life and its difficulties stopped her from reaching her potential. I aim to let my art enable me to become perhaps a teacher when we reach our destination."

"With your talent you can doubtless sell your work—or become a famous painter, such as the great Leonardo da Vinci, or even a later artist like Constable. Do you paint anything other than animals?"

She looked surprised that he knew of such artists. "Yes, but I could hardly bring my oils and easel along on the road could I now?" she asked with a small laugh. "I have to make do with my colouring pencils."

As she talked, she began to draw what he soon realised was a budgerigar, the small birds that at times flew in such large flocks it seemed like a cloud passing over the sun. Time seemed suspended as he watched, and only when he heard Carlos open the door to the room next door and call his name, did he realise that he must have sat here a very long time. She had yawned more than once. "I will leave you," he said rising. "Come Bracken, I will take you outside and I will then fetch you back to watch out for Jo." The dog wagged his tail as he followed Tim out.

As Tim went down the stairs, he noticed a figure lurking by the front door, but the passageway was so dim he could not tell if it was male or female as he continued out the back door. He used the privy while Bracken did what he needed to do, and then went back inside. The passageway was now empty, so he guessed the person must have been on their way out. Bracken beat him to Jo's door and stood with his tongue lolling, as he scratched a paw down the wooden panel.

"All right, boy, you have deserted me and are besotted by the wench, I know," he said as he rapped softly on the door panel. There was no answer so Tim imagined she must already be asleep. As silently as he could he opened the door wide enough for the dog to slip through. About to close the door after Bracken, he stopped in alarm when his dog began to snarl, a sound he rarely made. A growl of warning was usually the worst he managed to use to scare people off.

Tim called out, but got no answer from Jo, only a continued snarl from Bracken, so he pushed the door wider. Bracken stood atop a shape that was lying across the bed and beneath both of them was Jo. When the shape moved in an effort to shake off the dog, who now had his arm firmly in his grip, Jo began to scream. There was no doubt it was a man, and a large one at that. As Bracken's teeth dug deeper, his prey began to flounder about with his other arm in an effort to rid himself of his attacker.

Tim moved swiftly and pulled the figure off the bed and onto the floor where Bracken continued to cling to the arm where blood was now spurting. The man continued trying to shake him off, while cursing vilely. It was then Tim recognised him. "Archie!" he shouted.

Carlos then appeared at the doorway, rubbing his head, but when he took in the scene before him, stepped closer and stood above Archie, legs spread. "What the hell, man!" he yelled. "You had a choice of whores and harlots at the pub, why try to accost an innocent girl?"

"Innocent? She ain't no innocent is she, or else she wouldn't be a 'traveling along with a group of men, and aside a black fella at that." Archie waved the free arm again, slapping at Bracken who hung on resolutely. "Get yer stupid mutt off me."

Before Tim could react, Carlos brought his fist down on the side of Archie's head. When Tim gave Bracken the order to release the offender, Archie tried to scramble to his feet. But Carlos held him fast with a booted foot pressed to his chest, while Tim stood on the hand below the bleeding arm. Archie cried out in pain.

The owner of the house then appeared in the passageway, lamp held high. “What in heaven’s name is going on here?” he asked. “This is a respectable establishment, and I don’t hold with all this carry on.”

“Do you have a constable close at hand, or failing that can we send to the barracks for aid? This man was intending to force himself on this woman. Please be so kind as to send for someone to arrest this criminal,” Tim said.

Jo had pulled the cover over her shoulders, and now sat huddled against the wall, quietly weeping. Desperately wanting to comfort her, Tim knew that if he and Carlos stepped away, the culprit would hightail it out of there.

Rubbing his jaw, the proprietor looked perplexed. “I’ll send my lad off in the hope the constable is not out catching thieves. There’s a lot of sheep stealing been going on.” He glanced down at the now subdued Archie. “Can you keep him restrained a while?”

Carlos nodded. “Aye, have no fear, he isn’t about to go anywhere this night except to the lockup.”

After the owner went off and down the stairs, Carlos dragged Archie to his feet. He stumbled about and it was clear the man had taken too much gin or rum this night. “I’ll take him out of the way while you offer the wench comfort,” he said as he gave Archie a push in the back, warning, “Get out and don’t try anything stupid or I’ll give you a good going over.” Bracken followed close at Carlos’ heels, not about to let his prey far out of his sight.

Tim sat on the side of Jo’s bed, not knowing what to say. How did you offer comfort to a young woman in such distress? It was something he had never had cause to do. She was clearly still very upset although the tears had ceased. “Can I get you anything, water or perhaps I can ask if a mug of tea could be supplied.”

She shook her head. Tim realised that she wore a nightdress of some soft pale fabric. Apart from the one coverlet she held about her, the rest of the bedcovers lay on the floor. She pulled her knees up to her chin. “No, thank you, Tim, just stay with me a while please," she said in a quiet little voice, very unlike her usual self. She sounded unsure—not surprising after what she had experienced this night.

"Off course I will stay." He went over and closed the door. "Did you not have a bolt on here?" He tapped the lock. "I see there is no key."

Her head went from side to side. "I have not been accustomed to locking myself in. I am sorry, I didn't think it necessary while you were nearby."

"Thank God I was not further away." Tim shuddered at that thought. It was possible that he could have been detained in the garden, or elsewhere. "He must have followed Carlos across from the public house. I am afraid this could well not be the last of such criminal activity we will encounter along the way, Jo. I did warn you it was not a place for a female. And what of when we get further south, and the towns begin to grow sparser." He sighed. Not a lot to do about it now. There was no thought of sending her back—unless they encountered a party going north with military officers along for protection. No point in upsetting her more by suggesting such, and it was likely she knew full well her mistake.

"I have been foolish, Tim, and I apologise." She seemed tiny as she huddled in the corner against the wall, and Tim curbed a sudden desire to hold her and offer her comfort. Likely, she had suffered enough for one night with the attentions of a male and would not welcome his touch.

"No need." He shrugged as Carlos knocked on the door and then pushed it open.

"Well?" Tim asked.

"The constable was in the public house, so we were in luck. He has taken the offender off to the lock-up." Carlos looked from Tim and back to Jo. Bracken had followed him in and now sat beside Jo. He bent to pat his head, saying, "Good dog. What a to-do. Jacko will not be too pleased."

"I care not for what Jacko thinks. He should choose his helpers more wisely I feel." Tim stood, and stared down at the small woman still huddled on the bed, asking, "Will you be all right if we leave you now? Bracken will stay with you."

She nibbled on her lower lip, and then asked, "Do you think I might share with you?"

Tim looked at Carlos, unsure what to say in answer to that. Carlos saved him making a decision by saying, "You can sleep in my bed, Jo, and I will take yours. How does that suit? The night is well-nigh over now anyway, as we must be up at sunrise."

"Thank you." She pulled the blanket tighter about her and put her bare feet to the floor. "I would really like that. I fear I would not sleep another wink in this bed."

Tim gestured for her to go before him. With Bracken at her side, she went to the door. Before going out, Tim sent Carlos a small salute. Carlos grinned and flopped down on her bed.

Uncertainly she stood just inside the room and looked around. "Which one should I take?" she asked.

"Perhaps you will feel more secure with mine—it is away from the door." He pointed to his bed. "And mine has not been slept in." The covers on Carlos bed were rumpled.

"Thank you, Tim. You are a kind person, I am lucky to have you as a friend," she said as she lay back and pulled the covers over her.

Uncertain what to do, Tim lay on the top of the covers. Normally he slept in his under breeches, as most men did, but perhaps if he started to strip off, she might become wary, thinking he was just as bad as her attacker. He patted Bracken's head when his dog licked the hand hanging over the edge of the bed. Jo's soft and even breathing told him she was soon sleeping, but he had a feeling he would not get much sleep this night.

Chapter Five

“What do you mean—we should find another wagon team to accompany us on our journey?” In his anger, Tim’s voice rose. The sun was barely up when they arrived at the yards. Billy had already fed and watered their horses and the pack animals were loaded and ready to go, when Jacko stormed up to Tim and Carlos, delivering the news that with the woman along they were more nuisance than they were worth.

“For that silly chit I have lost one of my most reliable men,” he shouted, waving a fist in front of Carlos’s nose. “The constable refuses to release him, saying he must wait for the magistrate’s next sitting.”

“Reliable, are you mad? The man is a scoundrel and does not deserve to be released,” Tim shouted back. “He invaded the wench’s privacy and if we had not caught him before he went ahead with his assault, he would now be guilty of a far worse crime.”

“The woman has asked for trouble since joining our party in Sydney. The plan was for you two men to accompany us—not some frivolous woman who will no doubt cause trouble wherever she goes...” He paused. “...and then there’s her black fella.” He gestured towards Billy who stood silently watching.

“Bugger off then, if you feel so strongly about it. We need you not.” Tim waved a hand. “We will find another wagon to journey along with.”

Jacko swore and walked off to his wagon, where his other helpers stood, looking confused.

Carlos had been standing silently by. He pulled on Tim’s arm and said low, “Are you certain about this, Tim? Perhaps we should reason with him.”

“I doubt the man will listen to reason. If he sides in with that scoundrel instead of seeing that the man deserves to be behind bars, then I have no wish to have him as a travelling companion. Surely we will find another bullocky heading south.”

“Easier said than done, my boy.” Carlos walked over to his horse and checked the saddle and girth strap, thanked Billy for tending to the animals, and ensuring they were fed, and then went to sit atop a fence.

Jo stood aside through all this, stroking the neck of her horse. They all watched as Jacko and his two remaining helpers left. The younger fellow who had befriended Jo sent her a look of apology. Once the dust settled behind them, Tim took off his hat and banged it free of dust on his leg.

The yard was unusually quiet for this time of the morning, and only one other wagon stood nearby, currently not in use, its oxen still in a yard at the back. The bullocky gave them a look and a shrug of disinterest and walked off whistling. Little use asking him for assistance, Tim decided.

“Perhaps it would be best if Billy and I go alone from here,” Jo said. Tim was so angry at Jacko’s reasoning that he hadn’t noticed her at his side.

“And where pray will you go? You cannot travel this road alone with just Billy for company. What happens if another such as that rogue accosts you? It is dangerous enough for us men. Have you a rifle amid your packages?”

“Yes, of course. I was prepared for Billy hunting for us.” Her sweet mouth went down at the corners. “Believe it or not I was more concerned about a lack of food than being attacked.”

“Could be you should let her go her own way, Tim lad,” Carlos said from his seat on the fence. “When all is said and done, she has brought more trouble upon herself and therefore us, and we are barely into the start of our long journey.”

Now Tim’s anger was directed at his uncle. “So you are blaming her for being attacked by that scum Archie, are you? And the only other trouble was from a no-hoper sheep drover with little sense and decency."

"Of course she is not to be blamed for the attack, but I am just saying…"

Tim cut Carlos short by standing in front of him, waving a fist beneath his chin. "Saying what? A female cannot be civil to anyone without them thinking her forward? And anyway, if you hadn't taken yourself over to the public house last night none of this would have happened!"

"Now hang on a moment." Carlos dropped from the fence and stood nose to nose with Tim. "So now you are saying a man cannot have a drink or two with other fellows. I had little conversation with Archie." He looked down and for a moment looked uncertain. "Maybe I did happen to mention that we were lodging across the road. No doubt he followed me as we left the inn."

"No doubt." Tim walked away.

"Your uncle is likely right. I will only bring more problems upon you, I feel, and I do not wish to be the object of a rift between you two," Jo said as she twisted her hat in her hands. "I should never have decided upon my foolhardy actions."

"I grant it was foolhardy to plan to travel with us without our consent, Jo, but it would be even more foolhardy to go off alone now, and just where would you head for?" Tim asked, rubbing his forehead where a pain throbbed.

"I could perhaps get passage on a steamer going south."

"What, dressed as you are?" Tim sighed. "And what of Billy, would he go by boat also? You are now also responsible for him, you understand. There's a slight chance he might meet up with his own people, but we have not seen any natives so far, so it is possible they are keeping well away from this town and its white inhabitants."

She nibbled on her mouth. "I have money. My clothing is not a problem. There is a store in town is there not?"

Carlos had walked away a few paces. He came back and said, "I apologise for my remarks. Of course, there is no question of you going off alone, girl. I was rash, in a moment of thoughtlessness." He turned to Tim. "We could visit the barracks and find out if there are to be any parties travelling south that we could tag along with."

Tim considered that, before saying, "I think we should make for Campbell Town this day. The last survey report I read said that a successful coach service is now running to Bong Bong further south, and one to Appin commenced only recently, so there is a chance we will meet up with more travellers beyond Campbell Town, and it is just fourteen or so miles away. I reckon we can travel faster on our own and make it today. What do you think?"

Carlos nodded. "Let us get started."

After visiting the store and purchasing supplies, and ensuring the water carriers were all full, they set off. As luck would have it, the sun had decided to hide behind clouds, so the weather was pleasantly cool. A few miles out of town, they passed Jacko and his team of oxen. He ignored them as they rode on.

Jo said little, and Tim felt guilty that the wench had been made to feel unwanted and knew he was relieved to be away from Jacko. In hindsight, perhaps they would have been better suited to travelling alone anyway. A regular overland fortnightly postal service now ran between Port Philip and Sydney thanks to Joseph Hawdon who secured a Government contract. The mail was passed to one John Burke at Yass, and it was reported that in his first year he rode alone over ten thousand miles to ensure the mail was delivered. If one lone man could undertake such a journey then, surely, they could.

A dray laden with bales of wool was the only other traveller they passed in the first couple of hours. The bullocky waved and called out to them as he continued on, no doubt to the dock at Liverpool. At a creek, they let the horses and Bracken drink, ate bread and cheese, refreshed themselves and continued on their way. Bracken was now happy to spend part of the day atop one of the packhorses.

As they neared Campbell Town, a wagon drawn by two sturdy horses came towards them. As it drew near, the driver, a man of middle years, hailed them and halted. A lad of about twelve years sat at his side. The boy ignored them, but seemed interested in Bracken, sitting majestically atop the pack. After saying a cheerful hello, the man asked, "Are you looking for somewhere to set yourselves down for the night?" His broad accent said he was Irish.

"Well, we will be as we get nearer town," Tim said. "Can you recommend somewhere?"

"I can. I would welcome the payment. Better to give it to me than someone else. There ain't much on offer in town." He laughed heartily.

"Is there a safe yard for the horses?" Carlos asked.

"Most certainly. I have a small errand to finish for the good wife, and then I will be following you. Now, a mile or so ahead you will see our home set back on the side. Cannot miss it for 'tis on its own. Just tell the missus Rex sent you and she is to make you comfortable." He slapped the rein on the rump of one of the horses, said, "Giddup Jes," and continued on his way.

"Well, that's a turn up. What do you reckon?" Tim asked.

"Can't be any worse than the hostelry of last night." Carlos removed his hat and rubbed his head. "And I would say the man is in need of our money."

True to his word, they spotted his home, and turned off the road to follow a rutted track. A woman came from the house and hailed them. She looked to be about thirty years but with straggly hair and weary eyes, it was difficult to decipher her true age. A small girl clung to her skirts and a baby whimpered in the room behind her. She looked apprehensive, until Tim said, "Rex sent us—he said you would offer us somewhere to stay for the night. Of course, we will pay you for your hospitality."

"That's just like my Rex," she said with a smile. "You put your animals back there in the yard, and you will find water for them. Do you have fodder? We are short at the moment." She gestured beyond the house. A dog of mixed breed barked at them, and she said, “Never mind old Dingo here, he won’t do you any harm. Is your dog friendly?”

“Yes, Bracken is no worry. And yes, we do carry enough dry feed for the animals, thank you. Is there a store in town where we can stock up?”

“Oh yes, and we have a doctor, and our own superintendent of police, and if you wish to pray, St John’s church is recently opened.” All this she said with obvious pride. “An’ the boys go off to the schoolhouse for their learning. Once you settle the horses, come to the door and I will show you where you can sleep.” She went inside.

Billy was quite happy to stay with the horses again. The makeshift yard would not offer a lot of security and the small ramshackle shelter to one side, where they unloaded their packs, told them that this family were indeed in need of money. Tim was disappointed that the grass was sparse—it would have been good to let the horses graze.

Their poor circumstances were reinforced when she opened the door of a lean-to behind the house. “Where will the black lad sleep?” she asked as she stood back. Jo now had her hat in her hand and the woman put a hand to her mouth, saying, “Oh, I beg your pardon, miss. I thought you were a lad too. This is just like my fellow. I have no room inside the house, what with the youngsters all needing a place to lie down. I have four in there you see, and one is off out with Rex. I should have shown you the room before.”

What she showed them could never be termed a room. Gaps wide enough to poke a hand through peppered the walls, and the roof of straw looked ready to collapse in on them at any moment. Two narrow beds took up most of the space. Tim was sure he saw a large rat run across the dirt floor. Bracken also spied it, but it shot out through a gap in the wall before he could catch it.

Before Tim could answer, Jo said, “This will do fine, do not fret. We will be quite able to manage. Thank you for your kind hospitality. Do you have a pump, and a privy?”

“If you’re sure, my dear.” Tim thought she looked uncertain but relieved. “The pump is at the front. We are lucky—we have our town reservoir. Built by the convicts a while back. And the privy is yonder." She pointed to where a tiny shack stood a distance away from the house. "Rex dug the hole himself," she added as if that was important. "When he returns, we will have a meal. I only have stew, I am afraid, 'tis mighty hard to grow vegetables, but we make do." She left them.

Tim and Carlos stared at each other while Jo set her small bag down on a tree stump, the only other object that resembled furniture. "This family are in dire need of help," she said with a sigh. "That woman must have started having her babies when she was a child. I wonder if they came here as convicts, or thought that by settling here they would have a better life than back in their own country."

Tim shrugged. Jo seemed to be taking the fact lightly that there was not enough room for all three of them to sleep in this shack. The woman never ceased to amaze him. Unshocked by the conditions here, she was more concerned for the woman's difficult lot in life.

"I'll just… go and… and then find the pump," she said, waving towards the privy, before darting off, Bracken at her heels.

"I think it fortunate that there is not a gale blowing," Carlos said with a laugh. "Or that wooden excuse for a privy would not last long. So what are we going to do, young Tim? Two beds and three of us?"

Tim shook his head. "I have not a notion. Jo has the right of it—this family need our money so we must make do. I think we must sleep fully clothed this night, Carlos."

"I have an idea that is better. I will join Billy and sleep beneath the stars. 'Tis a fine night and not likely to rain. Won't be the first time or the last."

Not sure if he found the prospect of sharing with Jo daunting or otherwise, Tim said nothing.

Soon Rex returned, greeting them with pleasure. Once he had unharnessed his horses and put them in the yard alongside the other horses he said, "Come inside now, and share our meal, you too lad." He gestured to Billy who stood by the fence. They all followed him into the home that was simply one large room, with a loft above.

"Sit where you can," the woman said. Turning to the two eldest boys who were pushing at each other in their haste to gain a seat on the hard bench along the table's side, she scolded, "Sit and show your good manners lads, please."

Rex took the one rickety chair at the head of the table and waved them down. All four of them sat on the bench on the other side of the table. "Where will you sit, Madam?" Jo asked when it looked like there would not be enough room for her around the already crowded table.

"Do not fret, I will squeeze in along with the children—move along, pet," She pushed the girl, who seemed fascinated by the visitors, closer to the three boys. The baby lay in a rough-hewn box on the floor, happily chewing on a chunk of what looked like bread. The woman then ladled out stew onto tin plates and handed them around. Once all were served, she sat.

The stew was surprisingly tasty, and obviously had small portions of lamb in it. "So, kind folk, how did you come to be living in this part of the colony?" Tim asked.

"Well, me lad, 'tis a long and at times sorrowful story, but if you are really interested, I shall tell you." Rex finished his stew, congratulated his wife on a splendid meal and said, "I worked on the docks in Ireland as a lad. Of course, times were hard as you no doubt know, and I got caught as most did a' thieving to make some cash." He laughed.

"And you were transported for some petty crime?"

"Oh yes, and so I was eventually sent across the seas to this fair land." He glanced across at his wife. "I have no regrets. For 'twas up in Sydney Town I met my darling Marie here and was smitten. She came across with a family and worked in their house as a maid."

The children all asked if they could be excused, and when given permission, rowdily scampered outside. "Would your dog like a bone to chew on?" Marie asked. Tim thanked her and the two dogs went outside with their prize. Tim noted the bones had not a smidgen of meat left on them and so he would have to ensure Bracken got extra food tomorrow.

"Now, where was I?" Rex asked. "Ah yes, of course I couldn't ask for her hand as I was still a con, and anyway she wasn't of an age to wed."

"Who would like a cup of hot tea?" Marie asked, and after they all said they would she rose to brew it. The kettle sat atop a dilapidated stove.

"And so you had to wait until she was of the age of consent?" Carlos asked.

Rex looked shamefaced. "Unfortunately, we kind of put the cart before the horse and she was with child." He scratched his head, and grimaced. "This is where the tale starts to go downhill as they say. They sacked her, didn't they? Threw her out with just the clothes on her sweet back. What could we do but go to the priest and confess our misfortune? As luck would have it, he married us right away."

"And that is when you decided to head south, is it?" Jo asked. She had been listening to the tale with rounded eyes.

"Ah no, lass. We had to wait until I got me ticket of leave. By then our next son had arrived. I got work fine—and I tried me hand at bare fist fighting about then." His grin said he enjoyed the sport. "Made a penny or two at it, too. We were doing fine. Marie got herself a job doing housework now and then for a posh lady or two, an' with me fighting and doing odd jobs at the cattle yards we got by."

Tim had not taken a lot of notice of Rex's body but now realised that the man was sturdily built and so obviously had the physique of a fighter.

"When the talk started about how many men were upping sticks and heading down to the new colony at Port Philip, I met this bloke." He rubbed his chin. "Thought he was a good 'un didn't I? He was dead keen on getting a flock and trying his hand at sheep farming. Said he heard that once you found where you wanted to squat, all you had to do was claim your patch, pay the government for the licence, and so much for each animal, and then you could make a fortune. I decided to tag along. Of course, I never considered my family." He sent Marie a small smile of apology.

"Is he still in these parts?" Tim asked.

"No, his notion was to try for land around Naralling, and that's where he headed. I came to realise the man had little sense of droving, and less knowledge than the sheep, and we'd had enough of his promises. Moreover, I had never taken into account that I might be away from my family for weeks at a time tending the flock. We are good Christian folk and believe Our Lord God watches over us, so off we went to the priest again for help." He glanced around their home. "The kind man offered us this place, said we could stay here as long as The Lord wanted us to."

"And do you manage to find employment in town?"

"I do odd jobs for the priest and also the good doctor, and Marie here goes up and does cleaning for their lady wives, and also sewing. Her days working for the gentry served her well, for she learnt how they like things." He beamed at his wife in pride. "Now folks, where are you heading and what do you plan to do when you get there?" he asked.

"The aim is to reach Port Philip, but once there we will find out what is in store for us." Tim rubbed his hands together. "I was employed by the government in Sydney so if all else fails I can always find a position with them. I have a letter of recommendation if I need it."

"And what of you, lass?" Marie asked. "How do you come to be travelling with these gents—is one of them your husband?"

Jo blushed, and with a small laugh shook her hand in front of her face. "Oh no, the one I proposed to refused me, I am afraid, so I sort of loaded myself upon them with no real plans in mind."

"Refused you? A pretty girl like you, what is he, mad?" Rex asked with a laugh. Tim felt heat creep up his cheeks.

"And why are you travelling with them, fella?" Rex looked at Billy, saving her from answering that.

"I hope to find my people," Billy said quietly.

"Well, you may find some down south, but there aren't any left around these parts, lad, so they say. You are the first black fella we've seen since being here. Have you heard of the killings that went on between the settlers and your kind some years back? The ones who weren't slain by squatters and settlers died of diseases brought in by us white folk so 'tis said. Why aren't you already with your kin then? I heard that further north they still sometimes hold what they call corroborees."

"I was captured when young and spent some years with a family." Billy shrugged. "I ended up with the kinfolk of this young person and they treated me kindly." He gestured briefly towards Jo.

"And they taught you their language, I take it." Rex nodded.

"I owe all to this lady." Billy sent a smile Jo's way. "She let me share her lessons."

"And what did your family think of you setting out on such a journey?" Marie looked to Jo.

"My family were slain by bush rangers," Jo said quietly. "Billy is like kin to me as we grew up together."

"Oh dear, I am sorry." Marie rose and went to the door, where she called out to the children. After a while, they noisily came in.

The baby began to cry, so Tim got up and said, "We will leave you now. Thank you for your kindness. We will be on our way early in the morning."

"We're always up at daybreak, lad." Rex went to the shelf above the stove and took down a pipe, which he began to fill.

Outside, the cloudless sky was a mass of stars. At odds what to do next Tim was relieved when Jo yawned and admitted she was tired. "I'll let you get settled and try not to disturb you when I come in," he said.

Bracken followed her while she went to the ramshackle hut and then to the pump, where she gave him a drink of water. “Your dog seems to have deserted you in favour of his new mistress,” Carlos said, as he leant against the fence beside Tim.

“That’s a fact. She seems to have a way with her that Bracken likes.” Tim watched Jo as she went back to the small room behind the house. Bracken paused beside him, wagging his tail as if waiting on a word from him. “Go on, boy, stay with her. And watch out for rats,” he called as the dog dashed over, pushed at the rickety door and went inside.

“And what about you? Does she have a way that pleases you?”

Tim punched him gently on the arm. “Enough,” he said, walking off towards the privy. Carlos’ laughter followed him.

When he came back, Tim pushed at the door of the shack as gently as he could, and looked around its edge. Jo lay facing the wall. Bracken lay alongside her—lifting his head, before flopping back down again with a sigh. Relieved that she was obviously asleep, Tim sat on the other cot and pulled off his boots, and then his breeches and shirt.

About to lie down, he stopped short when she said, “I do hope there are not snakes in here.”

“Never fear, Bracken will inform you if one should dare show its head, and the same goes for rats, I think they will keep well out of his way.”

Surprising him, she turned and sat up. She wore her white nightgown and appeared to take no heed of him sitting on the side of his bed in his undergarment, as she said, “These good people are in sore need of assistance.”

“I know, but short of paying them for our stay and food, I fear there is little we can do, Jo.” Tim leaned over and turned the lamp down low, lest she saw the effect her nearness and their lack of clothing was having on him. There was still plenty of light coming in through the many holes in the walls and he could see her clearly, but his state of undress apparently affected her not, for she then pushed the thin coverlet back and sat facing him as she stroked Bracken's head.

"There is plenty we can do, Tim. I have been thinking—what would you think if I gave them some of my small store of gold."

Tim shook his head. "Out of the question, where would he spend it? They are obviously well known in this town, and folk would suspect them of thievery. Anyway, I thought you had traded most of your gold, and only carried money. And where have you all this treasure hidden may I ask?"

"No, you may not ask," she said pertly. "And I have not brought sacks of gold, but just a small amount for emergencies sake." She wiggled forward and because of the lack of space, her knees ended up almost touching his.

"And another thing." Tim tried to keep an even tone. The shafts of moonlight across her face made her appear like a woodland nymph. He coughed. It would not do to let her see that he had begun to sweat despite the coolness of the night. "They are proud folk, I think, and would not take kindly to charity."

"Nonsense." She waved that suggestion aside. "Are they not taking charity from the priest who has given them this filthy hovel to live in? Good gracious, I lived in better out at the mine." A rude sound came out of her mouth.

She had a point. "All right," He agreed. "But we will give them money, certainly not your gold."

"Thank you, but I would like it to be my money. Let me do this for them, please?"

Before Tim could utter a word of agreement or otherwise, she had moved forward onto her knees in front of him, and he simply sat there for a moment in disbelief as she reached up and touched his mouth with a fingertip. "It is my birthday tomorrow, which means I will be eighteen." She giggled softly. "That means that from now on you must treat me as an adult."

Reaching up, she placed her hands behind his head and pressed her lips to his. Defenceless, he pulled her to his chest and deepened the kiss. She made no effort to move away, instead wriggled closer. A feeling flooded his whole being such as he had never known before when her fingers caressed his bare back, and he could feel her breasts against his chest. He wanted her with every part of his being, but he mumbled against her mouth, "Jo. We must stop, or you know where this will lead."

With a little sigh, she sank back and put a small space between them, whispering, "You do not desire me?"

"Don't be foolish. It is obvious is it not? I am just a man and we have desires. You are playing at temptation are you not? I should think you well know where such games end up, and what the outcome will be."

"I did not see it as a game. If you tell me now that you have not the teeniest desire for me, then I will never bother you so again. We will continue as we have been—simply as friends who are at times irritated by each other."

Bracken chose that moment to put his wet nose between them, and she laughed. Tim pulled at her hands, saying, "Sit here beside me." She obeyed and continued to pat the dog's head. "I may not be a lot older than you, but perhaps I know more about life than you."

She shook her head. "Perhaps you do, Tim. Did you not see the love between our hosts? They cared not for rules and what others thought and yet remain steadfast even with the hardships they endure with this life. My mother and father were similar—she followed him to the back of beyond and stood by him and his foolish dreams." She placed a hand on his knee, and he trembled. "Do you not wish for a love such as this? A love where you simply throw caution to the winds and take whatever life gives you?"

"Of course I do, and I know what you mean. I was born well before my Ma and Papa were wed and so was Annie. They went through a mountain of problems before finally realising they were meant to be together, and their love endures." He rubbed his forehead. "But do you not see that one of us has to be sensible and see where recklessness would take us. Supposing you got with child?"

"You have not a romantic soul, Tim. I have decided I am glad you do not desire me." With a huff and a flounce, she got up and went back to her bed, faced the wall and pulled the cover over her. Bracken gave Tim a strange look before following her.

Problem now was, he did desire her, and ached with that desire. The thought entered his head that perhaps he was the foolish one. What would she do if he now joined her on her bed and confessed his love? But was this love he felt, or simply lust brought on by the closeness and willingness of her to give herself to him, regardless of the consequences? Not for the first time he knew deep down how different he was to most men. He doubted others would have been so reticent this night. However, life had taught him to be cautious—and as he flopped back onto the bed, he cursed this cautious nature.

When next Tim opened his eyes, light was already streaming in through the gaps. The other bed was empty, woman and dog gone, as was Jo's pack. He hastily pulled on his clothes and ran his fingers through his hair before dashing outside. The sun was barely up over the horizon. Jo stood by the fence, deep in conversation with Rex. Billy was in the process of preparing the horses, and Carlos stood at the pump sloshing water over his head, so Tim did the same.

"I fear I am a fool, Carlos," Tim said as he shook water from his hair, then bent to pat Bracken, who stood wagging his tail after drinking from the bucket beneath the pump.

"Well, that is no great secret." Carlos thought that amusing which annoyed Tim. "So what have you done now? Has it something to do with your night alone with the fetching wench?"

"It has, and 'tis more what I have not done, I fear."

That sparked Carlos' interest. He ran his hands down his sides and stood waiting. "Tell me."

"Jo is at times a foolish child and at other times has the wisdom of an adult. You would think that being reared in a house where women tended my every need, I would know something of their ways and foibles. First there was Thelma who died when I was small, then Gracie, Ma's sturdy shipboard friend, who took on my care." He shrugged.

"None of us do, dear fellow. We just amble though life in the hope that one of them will choose us above all others."

"I think you were right, and it seems she has chosen me." Tim nodded towards the woman still talking to their host. "She offered herself and I turned her down. Does this mean that I do not return her affection sufficiently?"

"Perhaps it means the opposite, and you care too much." Carlos strolled over to join the others, leaving Tim deeper in turmoil.

Tim followed Carlos, and Rex hailed him, saying, "Talk some sense into this lass, would you fella?"

"What has she done now?" Tim asked, sensing he knew the problem.

"She is after overpaying me for my hospitality, an' I will not have a bit of it. We are not thieves and scallywags and I did not invite you into our home to strip you of your hard-earned money."

Tim sighed. "I warned you." He shot Jo a look of reproof. "Give the good man what he asked for and let us be on our way."

Jo's mouth was set mutinously, and Tim knew a fight was likely to follow. "If you will not accept what I offer, perhaps I have a solution that might prove more to your liking," she said.

All of them, including Billy, awaited her next statement with interest. When she pointed to the wagon sitting alongside the yard, and asked, "Do you own that and your horses?" Tim wasn't sure who appeared to be more surprised.

"Why, yes," Rex said slowly. "I purchased it in Sydney Town before we set off on our travels. It was sorely needed to carry my family. Why do you ask?"

"Would you consider selling it to me? I grow weary with sitting atop a horse and feel I would be better suited to driving a wagon. We are only at the beginning of our long journey and I would welcome a covered wagon to shelter our packs should the weather turn stormy."

Rex stood scratching his chin. "But we would have no transport should we desire to move to another town."

"And are you likely to decide to travel more?" Jo looked around at the meagre yard and the ramshackle house his family called home. "You seem to be settled here and have all that you need. I fear if you go to another town you will not find another such as your priest who will assist you with lodging as this one has done."

Of course, she was right, Tim knew it as well as she. It was most likely this family would never have enough money set by to consider moving elsewhere. Jo now looked at him, a question in her eyes. Tim shrugged, asking, "Are you sure about this?" Her idea was not so foolish on second thoughts. They still had far to travel, and a covered wagon would suit their needs should they have to make camp. In addition, he had not missed her weariness at the end of the day.

"I am." She turned back to Rex. "I will pay you what it cost you and more. Or." She put a finger to her cheek. "Would you be prepared to take my pack horse and one other horse also? Our animals will certainly cost you less to feed than your plough horses. Your children can ride them if the need arises as they are trustworthy animals."

The chit had thought of everything. Now Tim shook his head as he and Carlos shared a look of amazement at her audacity. "Which other do you propose to offer in this exchange?" he asked.

"Would you be prepared to lose one of your pack horses? You would have no need for two if we acquire the wagon. If you are not agreeable then I will forsake my horse, or the one Billy rides."

"First we are to ensure that Rex is agreeable to this trade before we make further decisions."

She nodded. "Of course. Well, what do you think, sir? Should you discuss it with your good wife?"

Rex stood scratching his head as he mulled it over. "How much would you offer as well as the horses?" he finally asked, obviously in no hurry to ask his wife's opinion. Tim could almost see his mind working as he fathomed if this deal was worthwhile.

"What say you to thirty-five pounds?" she asked. Tim knew that was more than a fair price as that would be a year's pay for most single working men. For a moment, he thought Rex would begin to bargain, but then he held out his work-roughened hand and shook the one Jo offered.

"Tis a fair deal." Rex grinned.

Tim wasn't sure if it was or not as he had no idea what the wagon and two shire horses were worth, only knew the worth of his pack horse. "First I must check the soundness of your horses, Rex," he said.

After a thorough check of the animals in question, Tim could find no fault with them. The sturdy creatures would certainly have no trouble travelling the miles. He just hoped the wagon did not fall apart.

It took a while to get the horses in harness, and the wagon loaded. Tim gave up the packhorse he knew was older, and not as sturdy as the other, and secured the other behind the wagon along with Jo's horse. A fair chunk of the morning had passed by the time they were saying their goodbyes to Rex and his wife. Their older boys had already left for the schoolhouse.

Jo seemed to have no problem driving the two horses, and after a stop in the town to buy supplies, they were on the road again.

Chapter Six

Tim had to admire Jo's spirit. She handled the horses and wagon with expert ease. Bracken was happy to sit beside her part of the day, watching the world go by. When Tim congratulated her, she told him she had driven the wagon out at her parent's mine on numerous occasions. Because the two shire horses were placid creatures, they plodded along happily carrying what was now a heavy load. The two horses hitched to the wagon seemed content without the burdens on their backs.

Neither Tim nor Jo mentioned that kiss the night before last. Tim sensed she had decided to keep a distance from him. Her judgment on trading the wagon proved right, for it offered her good shelter when they made camp last night. Because of the late start, they decided to stop before crossing the mountains hated by the bullockies.

Today they were heading for the village at Stonequarry Creek, twenty-three miles or so from Campbell Town. During his time at the Government office, Tim heard that only recently the small settlement was renamed Picton in honour of an old friend of Governor Brisbane, and a privately-owned town would be built on the land of Major Antill, who received the first land grant in the area. Last year building allotments were offered for sale. Unfortunately, Mr. Harper, who offered the land for sale, died earlier this year, so Tim had no idea what they would find when they reached the village.

As they neared the town the road became busier, with a couple of bullock drays passing on their way north with their loads of wool. "I heard there is an inn here that was built a year or so ago," Tim said to Carlos who rode alongside him. "So with luck we might get to sleep in a decent bed this night."

Carlos nodded as he looked to the sky. "We were fortunate last night as the rain held off, but the sky promises wet weather ahead." His prediction proved right and just as they neared the town, the rain began.

They found the inn easily, as there were few other hostelries to be seen. The innkeeper was amiable and offered them shelter for their horses in the large barn behind the inn if they so wished. They could also purchase dry food for the animals. As always, Billy was more than happy to stay with the horses. Tim sensed he was more comfortable with the animals than with humans, for not more than a few words came out of his mouth during the long hours of riding. He obviously favoured the outdoors.

"The lady requires a separate room if you have one available," Tim said when they went back into the bar. The innkeeper seemed unconcerned that Jo did not look one bit like a lady. Doubtless he was well used to all types passing through.

Once they had paid and arranged food for Billy and Bracken, the innkeeper said, "You can have your meal any time that suits." This time Jo put up no argument about paying her share, and said nothing as she was shown into her small room alongside Tim and Carlos' by a maid who offered hot water if needed.

"We will go down for a meal as soon as you are refreshed," Tim said to her, and received a small nod in response. When Carlos was out of earshot, he added, "Are we not to exchange civil words any more?"

"Of course, do not be foolish." Once she ensured Bracken was inside with her, she closed the door. Childish Tim knew, but the fact that his faithful hound had apparently chosen her over him, riled him.

The meal was well cooked and tasty. There were two others in the bar, a woman and a lad who looked to be of similar age to Jo or perhaps younger. The strapping boy ate heartily, saying little to the woman, obviously his mother.

“A fine looking female.” Carlos nodded towards them on the other side of the room. “Tis strange for a woman to be travelling alone—I wonder if she has a husband in town.” The twinkle in his eye suggested he hoped she was without a husband.

“Could be she is a widow.” There was little doubt that she was fair to look at—and probably of similar age to Carlos. Her clothes looked shabby, but that could be down to travelling. “We saw no other horses or wagon so perhaps she lives here—or is waiting for someone.” Jet-black hair was swept back neatly into a roll behind her head, held in place by an elaborate jewelled clasp. Her looks were surely striking, and when she looked their way, he saw that her eyes were her best feature. “She seems to find you as fascinating as you find her.” Tim chuckled.

“I appreciate the charm of a beautiful woman.” Carlos waved Tim’s suggestion aside.

“She is very attractive,” Jo said. “And the man with her is also handsome.”

“That is no man, but a mere lad.”

Jo made one of her rude noises at Tim’s remark. When the boy pushed back his chair and stood, she said, “In that case he is a big lad, for I swear he must be as tall as you.”

He did not attempt to assist the woman with her chair, so it looked likely that they were not highborn. After shaking out her skirts, she sent a small wave towards their table before sauntering across, a smile on her beautiful face.

As soon as the first word was out of her mouth, it was obvious that she came from the same part of London where many of the convicts sent to this land came from. Gracie, his Ma’s old shipboard friend and faithful helper over the years had the same way of speaking. Even Carlos and Mama still held traces in their speech of their early years spent in Stepney.

“Pleased to meet you.” She held out a be-ringed hand. “Are you people from hereabouts or travelling through?” Tim thought that rather forward for a woman alone, but

Carlos seemed unconcerned as he rose and took her hand in his.

"We are on our way south," he said with a smile fit to charm anyone. "And what of you, are you awaiting someone?"

"No." There seemed to be a trace of hesitancy in that one word. "I'm Winifred by the way, and this here is my boy Gilbert." With a small gesture, she included the boy who seemed to have his gaze fixed on Jo, which made Tim uneasy. "Everyone calls me Winnie or Win." There was still no real answer to Carlos' query.

Carlos pointed to Jo, saying, "Pleased to meet you, and this here is Jo. I'm Carlos, and this is my nephew Timothy, known by all as Tim."

"Charmed I'm sure." She hovered as if she expected more, so remembering the manners taught him, Tim rose and said, "May I offer you a seat?" As she thanked him and sat, he found a stool and pulled that alongside the table. She made no attempt to seat the lad, so Tim left him standing.

"Can I get you and Gilbert a drink—ale or wine, they serve both?" Carlos asked.

"Thank you kindly, I'll have a beer but none for him." She nodded to her boy, and with a hand next to her mouth said softly, "You'll have to forgive him, he has little or no speech."

The lad was looking down at Bracken, now sniffing his trouser leg, but did not attempt to pat the dog or move. Tim made the assumption Gilbert was slow witted.

Once their ordered drinks were brought to the table, Carlos asked again, "So what brings you to this outpost? Do you live in these parts, Winnie?"

"Bless you no." She gave his arm a small nudge. "It's a long and sorry tale I have to tell." Turning to her son she ordered, "Go outside and find the privy, lad." He obeyed and ambled off. When the back door had slammed after him, she said, "As you no doubt realise, he is not of sound mind, poor boy."

"Oh, I am sorry to hear that, Madam. Has he always been so?" Carlos face showed his pity.

"Well, he's not always been the brightest boy, and could not attend school, but his father…" Her face crumpled and she pulled out a scrap of cloth to mop at her eyes. Carlos patted her hand.

Tim now wondered if she was an out of work actress—but if that were so, why would she be so far from Sydney?

"And where is his father?" Carlos asked, looking about as if expecting to see the man suddenly appear. "Is he here, along with you?"

Her head went from side to side. "Dear me no. I escaped his clutches and ran away, taking the boy with me when he bashed poor Gilbert so badly he grew even worse, barely speaking at all."

"That is criminal." Carlos looked as shocked as Tim felt and Jo was chewing on her bottom lip, perhaps in fear that the brute had followed them. "Did you report this crime?"

"Good lord no, the constable was of the mind that he was a good sort and would never have believed he could treat his son so."

"How did you become wed to such a man? Surely you knew his type. Did you meet here or back in the old country?" Tim asked. Sadly, the colony was littered with failed marriages such as hers. Many women were forced to accept the offers of men, else live in poverty if they could not find employment.

"I met him on the ship coming over. He is of Germanic descent and is a handsome man. I was bowled over—just as many other women are—by looks rather than the person inside. My son is not unlike his father in appearance." She sighed loudly. "Sadly, I soon discovered he was a worthless layabout who preferred the booze to a good day's work. It was too much to bear though, when he started bashing Gilbert, for little but the lad being there. It is no wonder my boy is as he is. And truth is, we were never wed by a priest, so he has no real claim on me or his son." Her shrug spoke volumes. "With luck he will be glad to be rid of us."

Tim doubted that. He knew the type well and fancied the brute would not take lightly to being tossed aside. "But you still haven't explained how you come to be here, so many miles from town?"

She looked at Tim and seemed hesitant, before saying, "I managed to get us a lift with a party travelling south. I was simply intent on getting as far away as possible as fast as I could and didn't take into account the many miles between settlements. It's unfortunate they finished their journey in Campbell Town, and so I managed to get us another ride with a bullock driver to here, hoping to pick up someone willing to take us further south."

So, that was out. What had occurred to Tim early on in her tale was fact. She was after transport to Port Philip. "But what if your attacker happens to trail you? He could be after you already."

She shook her head. "He was full of the booze when we left in the night carrying as small a load as we could. It will take him a long time to work out where we are—doubtless, he is searching Sydney Town still. It would not occur to him that I would have the wit to get a ride out of town."

"And you are asking now if you and your boy can join us on this long and tedious journey?" Carlos asked.

She turned a beseeching gaze on him and asked, "Would you show such kindness? I have money—not a fortune, but I can pay our lodging along the road if needs be. And I am not a bad cook if you need such. I hope to get work down south. They say the new colony of Port Philip is about to thrive."

Carlos looked to Tim, a question in his eyes. "Would you leave us so that we can consider?" Tim said. "We are to assume you have little but what you can carry in a bag."

Standing, she grabbed his hand and shook it. "Thank you kindly. I will see what Gil is up to out there for so long. And yes, I have but a change of clothing for us and a few small necessities a woman needs to carry." She smiled across at Jo who had said nothing through this exchange, obviously appealing to the view of another female.

When she had gone Tim said, "Well, what do you say? It is obvious you are bowled over by her looks, dear uncle, so it is now up to you, Jo. I doubt she can ride so she would be sharing the wagon with you. The boy can ride one of the spare horses."

"I like her." Jo nodded. "And it would be pleasant to have the company of another woman. I miss my faithful companion and teacher… and I miss my mother."

That was something Tim had not taken into account. A woman alone travelling with men would indeed find many aspects disadvantageous. "So, it looks as if we vote for them to travel along with us."

Carlos rose and rubbed his hands together, saying, "I will tell the dear lady."

As Carlos hastened from the bar, Tim asked, "You are sure of this, Jo?"

"Yes. I feel sympathy for her, and her son is obviously in need of help."

"But what will we do if the son possesses traits passed down from his father? Will you feel so kindly towards him if he turns out to be a brute?"

"Let us treat him as if he is a poor defenceless soul who has been mistreated and if it turns out differently, then we can always leave them at another town along the way. I am certain he is no match for you and Carlos, should he become a nuisance." She stood. "I too need to go outside. Bracken will accompany me I am certain."

"I will join you."

Carlos and Winnie were leaning against the barn wall deep in conversation. Carlos hailed Tim and said, "The boy is curled up on the straw along with Billy. The pair are as comfy as a pair of lambs. Winnie says that he likes horses, which is good is it not?"

Tim nodded, hoping that Carlos was not about to make a fool of himself. For all they knew this woman could be a thief or might possibly have murdered the man she left behind. He felt a sense of relief that her son would be sleeping in the barn and not inside. The lad had shown a great deal of interest in Jo, which did not wholly please Tim.

* * *

“Are you certain the lad is happy to walk?” Tim asked. Jo had offered him her horse and saddle when they were preparing for the road at daybreak, but his mother said the boy could comfortably walk twenty miles a day if need be.

“I doubt he will complain—as I told you, my boy has little to say,” Winnie had said. “He was a happy baby, but when his father began to beat him for no reason, he went quiet like this.”

As they left the inn behind, Carlos said, “It is no wonder the lad is sturdy, his legs must be strong as trees.” He glanced about at the surrounding grassland. “There is not much of a town here, is there?”

“I asked the landlord why he decided to set up his business here,” Tim said. “He gets a good trade from passing travellers but is assured this town will be flourishing in no time. Forty-five parcels of land were advertised just recently and the Village of Picton, as it will be called, will be a private township, so he says.”

“Would be nice to own so much land, would it not?” Carlos looked to the horizon.

“For sure, but then there is the worry of drought and fires. Pa is always complaining about the responsibilities that go along with sheep farming.” Tim gestured towards the wagon, where the two women were laughing and chattering. “Seems our Jo is happy to have another female along. Why is it that women always seem to find a lot to discuss when they are together?”

“I have yet to work that out, Tim, my boy. It is my guess they spend a lot of time finding fault with us men and our foolish ways.” Carlos laughed.

“You are taken with Winifred are you not?”

“I like the lady. She is not one to put on airs, and that suits me fine. Do you have doubts still about us allowing them along?”

Tim scratched his chin where he could feel the roughness of the first signs of a beard. “People have a way of not always turning out to be as they first appear, so I will hold my opinion until I am shown they can be trustworthy. I can understand why she holds you in fascination but that is my main worry—outward beauty is oft times not the best judge of a person's character. But I hope for your sake I am being over cautious, Carlos." His uncle deserved to share his life with a decent woman.

"So, where are we heading today, Tim?"

"I would have liked to make it as far as Sutton Forest or even Bong Bong, but I fear we will not cover such a distance in one day, so when we tire, or the sun begins to set, we will either stop at the first inn we come across or make camp aside a creek. I am in need of a bath, and you are beginning to smell worse than the animal you ride." To prove his point Tim held his nose.

Carlos reached out to punch him on the arm but missed. "I see your point, lad, for I thought that was your horse making a stink from his arse, but it must have been you."

Jo glanced around, probably wondering what they were laughing about. "I have to admit the wench has surprised me," Tim said. "She certainly has a strength in her that you would not reckon by the size of her." She could do a hard day's work but certainly did not have the body of a miner or bullocky. Tim still wondered if they would ever get back onto the friendly footing they shared, before he stupidly turned her down. Carlos was of the opinion he was mad not to accept her offer, but Tim knew deep inside he would never forgive himself if she soon regretted her rash decision.

His Pa taught him from an early age that the women in your life must be treated with respect at all times. Tim never knew the true story of what happened between him and Ma before they finally wed, but even at an early age, he always sensed a passion between them. They certainly argued a lot, even now, despite the obvious love they shared. "Did Tiger ever talk about the early convict years while you were working over there?" he asked.

Carlos shrugged. "He told Remy more than me. I know he was just twelve when the buggers transported him for petty thievery, same as all of us. He won big at the gaming table and bought his first farm. He purchased his first flock from Governor Macquarie but had a yen to cross over the mountains, which he did after he and your Ma met. He has been successful, and I hope for their sake the success continues, but I fear the sheep trade is not as profitable as it was a few years back, and so this is why I would never hope to own a large spread. We could open a trading store as Remy did once we reach our destination, what say you to that, Tim?"

"I say, let us wait and see how the land lies, Carlos. We might get there and find numerous opportunities to become wealthy." They laughed heartily at that prospect.

The sun was high above them when they came across a creek fit for swimming. Carlos, Tim and Billy stripped off their shirts and breeches, and all laughed as Gilbert pulled off his boots before jumping in fully clothed. "Thank the lord the sun is out today, boy, or you would be very uncomfortable for the remainder of the day," Tim said. Gilbert laughed for the first time as, unconcerned, he splashed about like a child.

"Are you certain you will not join us, ladies?" Carlos called. "It is refreshingly cool in here."

Winifred came and stood on the nearest bank, shouting, "I took advantage of the offer of hot water for bathing last night thank you, gents. And I believe Jo did the same." She returned to where they had a small fire going and the billy on the boil above it.

Tim admitted privately that he was disappointed that Jo was not joining in their fun and had a feeling she would have enjoyed a frolic in the water. But there would be other times. Once they were told that the tea was brewed, Carlos and Tim climbed out and shook themselves, but the boys stayed in. Once Tim had pulled his breeches and boots on, he said, "Billy seems content to have a boy of similar age, and manner along. I notice the pair of them say little to each other but seem to get on well." Sitting beside Jo, he took the bread and chunk of meat she offered. They were fortunate in getting a freshly baked loaf from the inn, and of course, mutton was readily available.

He noticed that Jo was looking everywhere but at his naked chest and wondered if it bothered her that he was not fully clothed. "Winnie said that Gilbert cannot read or write, is that not sad? I will offer to teach him if he is willing to learn," she said.

"If he is willing to learn, then go ahead and try—that is all you can do. But be careful, Jo, the lad is already paying you a lot of attention of the kind you may not welcome."

"It is pleasant to know that someone finds me attractive enough to pay me attention," she snapped before jumping to her feet and going to the back of the wagon where she proceeded to rummage around.

Following her, Tim stood beside her, but she continued with her foolish foraging. He placed a hand over one of hers. "Be still woman, I did not refuse you because I find you unattractive—far from it, you are beautiful. Can you not see that I stopped us from doing something you might regret later?"

"You seem to forget, Timothy Carstairs, that I am not a child, and have a mind of my own, a mind that will choose who I give myself to and who I choose to disregard." She brought out a book from her pack and stalked back to flop down beside the river.

That was for certain, she had proved beyond all doubts she had a mind of her own and a stubborn one at that. Tim was not about to remind her about Archie and the fact that some men would take what they saw as rightfully theirs, whether they gained consent or not.

The lads were out of the water now and running around in an effort to dry off. Billy then pulled his clothes on. The saddle horses were busily grazing on the lush riverside grass, but the two wagon horses had not been unharnessed. Billy began to pull up tufts to feed to them, and Gilbert followed him and did the same. Carlos and Winnie were laughing and chatting easily as they ate their meal a short distance away.

Tim sat beside Jo and looked over her shoulder at the book she had open. It was a collection of art. She folded back the cover to show him that it was produced by John Gould and contained beautiful depictions of birds and animals native to this land. “One of my treasured possessions,” she said.

Gilbert seemed to lose interest in the horses and was now looking Jo’s way. He ambled over and with a sigh sank down beside her. When she asked, “You like the pictures?” he nodded vigorously as he pointed to a drawing. “Kangaroo,” she said, and he nodded some more. “Would you like to learn how to read the words?” she asked. Agape he looked at her, a small smile twisting his mouth.

Winnie chose that moment to call out, “Eat your food, Gil,” and he jumped up and walked across to stand above her.

Tim stood, brushing at his rear, saying, “It is time to move,” and the others did the same.

They passed no inns or likely places to lodge for the night, so at nightfall made camp in the shelter of a stand of coolabah trees. When Jo brought out her book again, Gilbert showed more interest in the pictures than the words. When she opened the pad she used for her sketches and began to start showing him the letters of the alphabet, Tim commented, “I fear you have a long job on your hands.”

“We have time,” she said. “I remember my dear Matilda telling me that some of the children she taught in her early days as a governess were of wealthy families but held no interest whatsoever in learning. It is all in repetition, she told me.”

Tim admired her dedication to the task she had set herself. As it drew near time to retire Carlos followed Tim when he went off behind a tree some distance away. They stood side by side to relieve themselves and Carlos said low, “How would you like to share your tent with your fair Jo? Winnie is agreeable to sharing with me, and Gilbert seems quite happy to lie in the open with Billy. If it should rain, they have the wagon for shelter.”

"You do not waste your time, do you Uncle?" Tim laughed at Carlos' audacity.

"I am no fool and the lady is quite amenable." Carlos also chuckled. "Perhaps her willingness will spur your fair Jo to be the same."

"She most certainly is not *my* Jo as you put it and has now made it clear that she does not wish to spend any more time in my poor company than she must." Privately Tim was excited at the prospect and wished for it to rain so she would willingly seek shelter with him. "I leave it to you to put the suggestion to the young lady, so that she knows where it came from and is assured it is not from me."

"Fair enough, young Tim, leave it to me, I have a way with the ladies that they find hard to resist." He walked off towards Jo, who was in the act of storing her precious books away in the wagon.

"I will not!" This was said loud enough for all to hear, proving Carlos was not quite as charming as he imagined himself to be. "Whose idea is this may I ask?" Tim almost laughed aloud at her retort. The fair Jo was no easy conquest.

Carlos took her by the arm and led her a short distance away, so Tim was unable to hear their conversation, which then seemed to go on for a long time. He busied himself, ensuring the horses were secured safely in the makeshift yard they had set up using ropes around the trees. Tim knew his own horse would not wander off but was still uncertain of the large shires that pulled the wagon. The mare, Jes, was an amenable creature, and her younger companion seemed to follow her lead, but at times could be moody.

"I agree—on one condition." Jo stood above him as he bent to duck under the rope, startling him.

"Whatever you wish, Madam." Tim bowed low, and she sniffed haughtily.

"My wish does not seem to make the slightest difference where you and your conniving uncle are concerned," she snapped.

"You are becoming a shrew." He walked towards his tent and she followed. A few drops of rain began to fall as he ducked inside, Bracken at his heels. "So, tell me, what is your condition?" he asked as she tossed her small pack into the tent behind him and bent to enter.

While Tim sat on his sleeping sack and took off his boots, she crawled onto Carlos bedroll, also removing her boots. There was just enough moonlight streaking in through the flap to offer some light for him to see her shape but not her expression. "Well," he prompted, as she seemed to have forgotten her condition as she wriggled beneath the top cover and began to remove her breeches, with great difficulty. She obviously did not intend to sleep fully clothed, so he stripped off his breeches and tossed his shirt aside. Bracken immediately made himself a comfortable spot upon the bottom of her bed, turning a few times before letting out a satisfied grunt.

"It is not worth mentioning, so I am content to sleep and pretend I am alone." She shuffled down further and removed her shirt. "I trust you will be a gentleman and not take advantage of me."

Halfway beneath the cover, Tim sat up again and let out a laugh. "If I recall correctly Madam Jo, it was not I who took advantage of you, but the other way around. Perhaps if I had not been such a fool we would not now be at such odds." He lay back down and let out a huge sigh. "I do not understand you women at all. Do any of you really know what you want from us men? Winnie has obviously made her decision within a short space of time and Carlos is of course happy. He has maturity on his side. It is a known fact that we men are stupidly ignorant of what pleases a woman—goodnight and sweet dreams," he finished with a huff, as he turned away from her and pulled the cover over his shoulders.

There was no answer from her, and before long, her even snuffling said she was asleep. Tim found it harder to find rest and lay for a while with his hands beneath his head, listening to the rain on the tent and the wind rustling through the trees. He hoped the lads had the sense to climb atop the wagon and take shelter.

As a clap of thunder rolled across right above them, Jo's scream brought Tim out of his slumber. She was sitting up and sobbing. Tim climbed out of his bedroll and knelt beside her, asking, "What is it?" as he stroked her arm. "I think you were having a bad dream."

"I'm sorry," she muttered. "I thought I was forgetting, but the thunder brings back all the awful memories."

"Tis I who am sorry, Jo. I forget at times that you went through such horrors. To see all your loved ones taken from you while you had to witness such a crime, and be useless to offer aid, must have been worse than a nightmare. I can't imagine how I would live with such memories."

Her sobs had turned to quiet sniffles, and she touched his bristly chin. "I cannot expect you to share my grief. It is something I will have to carry with me forever. People say that time will heal the wounds, but who knows the truth of it." Her shoulders lifted in a shrug.

"Can you get back to sleep or would you like to talk awhile?" he asked as he went back on his heels.

"I doubt I will sleep much more this night." She gave a small laugh as Bracken licked her hand. "Good boy, you go back to sleep." He obeyed and did his usual few turns before flopping down, this time closer to her and taking up a good deal of the bed space. "Your dog has stolen my bed—I have not room to stretch out," she complained.

Tim returned to his bedroll and hesitated a second before suggesting, "Would you care to share mine, it is not roomy but at least your legs will not need to be cramped up—simply for comfort you understand," he added hastily, not wishing to ruin the sense of friendship they seem to have re-found. "I have been told that in times of stress it is a great help to have someone offer you a comforting arm to lean on."

"You are very kind." Tim noted a touch of sarcasm in that response and thought perhaps his offer would be rejected, but after a moment when he could hear her scuffling about, she gave him a gentle push on the arm, and he moved over.

She now wore her nightgown, he noted, which she pulled down after settling beside him. As he said, there was barely room for two, and as she fidgeted to get comfortable, the response of his body was immediate. "I'm sorry," he muttered.

"I take it as a compliment," she said, a smile in her voice.

There was little doubt that this woman was unlike any other. Would he ever learn to understand her? Not daring to touch her, he lay stiffly. Because of the lack of space, he could do nothing but lie on his side, so his entire body was in contact with her warm back, and his under breeches and her nightgown were little barrier between them.

"Most women do not wish for much out of life and men," she said in a soft voice. "Kindness would be at the top of my list of absolute essentials I would demand from the man I chose to love. My mother told me that if a man is kind, most women could forgive him for his many faults. I think you are a kind person Tim. Another thing my mother taught me is that you can be sure a man who is kind to his animals and puts their welfare ahead of his own needs, is a good-hearted man."

As she spoke, she ran her fingers down his arm and when she reached his hand, she pulled it across her until he could do nothing but wrap her close, his arm beneath her full breasts. She sighed and snuggled closer, if that was possible, in the cramped space. "Goodnight," she whispered.

Every part of his body felt a tingle, from his scalp to his toes. The thought of getting any sleep this night was out of the question.

Chapter Seven

"Are you asleep?" Her whispered question startled him, for he had thought her asleep when her breathing became steady.

"To be honest, Josephine, dear girl, sleep is impossible with you so near," he murmured.

"Am I really—your dear girl?" she shuffled over until she lay on her back. The wind had dropped and the only sound now, apart from the rain, was Bracken's snoring. Her movement had brought his arm in closer contact with her breasts so that he could feel their fullness and the tips like pebbles.

"Jo." There was warning in that one word. His body was already as hot as coals despite the fact that it was a cool night.

"I came into your bed at your invitation," she said next to his ear so that her warm breath fanned his skin.

"You have the soul of a temptress, Madam." Of its own accord, the hand across her found a breast and began to stroke it. "I am a mere man, and your actions can only result in one thing."

"Perhaps I wish it as much as you. Help me forget the horrors I experienced, Tim, love me, please?"

Tim groaned at her soft plea. "Sometime in the future, when you are cursing me, remember it was your wish," he whispered in the second before their lips met. She tasted like heaven and everything sweet in this life. His whole being became immersed in the feelings her honeyed mouth evoked in him. He shifted until she was half beneath him, his left leg between hers. At her small groan, Bracken awoke and came to press his wet nose on Tim's shoulder.

When Tim softly told him, "I am not hurting her, boy," he went back to his slumber.

"Promise me, you will never hurt me, Tim," Jo whispered against his neck.

"Never willingly," he promised, adding a fervent hope to himself. Somewhere at the back of his mind was a small notion that he'd heard that the first time could be painful for a woman, but nothing on this earth would stop him now.

With every part of him, he wanted her as he had never wanted anything in this life before. "Can we remove this?" he pulled at the soft cloth of her nightgown, and she lifted her hips to free it. Tim pulled it up and over her head, tossing it aside, along with his under breeches. She wriggled free of her drawers, and they joined the discarded clothing.

His mouth moved and found a breast, and her soft moans told him this brought her pleasure. Her small hands, slightly roughened by pulling on the reins, began to travel over his chest. She found one of his nipples and copied his movements, then tentatively she moved her fingers lower until she touched the part of him that now pulsed with his desire. "Jo, I think we have to slow down, or this will be over too soon," he said on a small groan.

Her small laugh vibrated against his chest, as she wrapped her hand around the length of his arousal and squeezed. "I never realised," she said.

"Realized what, love? That you could drive me mad with your touch?"

"No, that I had the power to do such as this to you. Do I really drive you mad?" As if to emphasize her soft words, she began to move her fingers. Tim caught her by the wrist, and she stopped, but continued to press kisses on his chest.

"Mad with desire," he groaned, moving to touch her where he had touched no woman before. Her small jump of surprise, or pleasure, showed him she liked that as much as he did as she whispered his name against the hairs on his chest. Tim took her in his arms and moved her until she lay beneath him. “I wish the night was lighter so that I could see your face.”

Without hesitation, she wrapped her legs about him, and he could do nothing but enter her sweet welcoming body. Unfortunately, too soon her pleasure did not match his, and at her small cry of distress he halted his movements, whispering, “Sorry,” but was unable to stop.

As he rolled off her, she touched his mouth, saying, “It’s all right, Tim. I did not expect so much pain, but my mother taught me that a small amount of pain must be suffered throughout life so that we can then rejoice at the pleasure we gain along the way.”

“You are an incredible woman, Josephine, do you know that? It is I and not you who should be consoling you for the pain I caused. Now I feel guilty.” He pressed a kiss on her forehead.

“I have a feeling it does get better—or so I have been led to believe,” she said with a small giggle. “It is a shame we are here in this tent and not at an inn, as I have a feeling it would be nice to share a warm bath with you right now.”

“There is a river not far away—perhaps we should jump in there, naked as we are.”

“Nothing would be finer—if we were alone, but I fear Gilbert and Billy would soon be awake and watching.” She gave a small shiver. “And at least here I have your warmth to keep me from the cold.” She snuggled up to him, and Tim could not keep his eyes from drifting closed. As sleep claimed him, he thought how wonderful it was to sleep with her in his arms.

Tim sat up with a jolt. He was alone, even Bracken was missing, and for the first time in his life he felt lonely. How could one small woman make an adult male feel like a child who had lost his favourite cuddly toy? Daylight was just streaking across the sky as the sun weakly tried to warm the morning.

The tent flap was open so he peered out and could see Jo and Winnie further up the river, close to the bank where it was shallow. Jo had her nightgown held high to keep it from the water, and Winnie wore some sort of garment on her top half. The pair had their heads close and seemed to be deep in discussion. Carlos was further up the river in the opposite direction. Tim picked up his clothing from the floor and with it held in front of him, dashed for the water and threw it down on the bank before plunging in headfirst. The chill took his breath clean away for an instant. Bracken sensed a game and came swimming over, barking.

When he resurfaced, Tim was pleased to see that Billy was showing Gilbert how to harness the shires to the wagon, therefore they did not see the women as they hastily scrambled from the river to run behind a handy shrub. Bracken, seeing that Jo was out of the water, clambered out to follow her. Tim heard a squeal from behind the bush as the dog shook himself dry.

Tim was soon out of the water himself and dragging on his clothing. By the time the women appeared, fully clothed, Carlos was also dressed. Tim desperately wanted to get Jo alone, but once they had eaten a breakfast of bread, mutton and wild berries Billy had picked along the way, it was time to pack up their tents and be on the road.

The few times he caught Jo's eye, she blushed and looked away and he sincerely hoped she was not ashamed of what had happened. For himself, he felt unusually joyful. His good humour must have been obvious, for once they were all mounted and away, Carlos rode to his side and asked with a laugh, "Your night went well, young Tim?"

Tim felt colour flush his cheeks, making him feel foolish, as he replied, "Never better, Carlos, and I trust your lady was as you expected?"

"Oh yes, and more." Carlos chuckled heartily and they rode in silence for a while, until Carlos said, "I think I will marry this woman."

"Good God man, you have only just met her, and for all you know she could well be still wed to the father of Gilbert there." He gestured towards the boy, now trotting along beside the wagon. The lad possessed so much strength it was frightening.

"She assures me there was no ceremony, and I believe her." Carlos shrugged. "We have to believe in people at some point in life, do we not? I choose to believe she is free and as eager as I to be wed. So, we will do the deed when we reach the next church or chapel and find a willing man of God."

Tim shook his head, knowing there was little point in arguing further. Carlos was mature and old enough to know his own mind. A thought entered his head then, could the fair Josephine now have marriage in mind? Moreover, if she did, would he be willing to agree. The thought of spending every night in her arms appealed, as he never imagined it might. He knew her well, and despite her at times stubborn ways, she was a beautiful and talented woman. "Should I propose marriage to Jo?" he blurted without thinking, and Carlos stared at him in obvious surprise.

"Why?" was his reply. "You are young and have many years of frolicking ahead, lad, so don't mistake one night of passion for a lasting love."

"But is that not what you have done?" It was Tim's turn to stare at his uncle. "I at least have known Josephine for a year or more and spent many pleasant hours in her company, whereas you must barely know this woman you intend tying yourself to."

"I have tested the waters, Tim, and know more about women than I guess you do and consider I could do much worse." He patted the neck of the horse beneath him in thought, and then said, "I simply feel it is the right thing to do."

"And what of her son?" Tim nodded towards the plodding Gilbert, wondering what the lad thought of his mother sharing a tent with Carlos. Tim caught him once or twice earlier in the day watching Carlos with a frown on his face. "What if he objects to this match?"

"He may be larger than the average man and indeed coming up to manhood, but I feel he is childlike and will do what his mother orders him to do. If I treat him kindly and show I am unlike the brute of a father they left behind, then he will grow to like me."

Tim certainly hoped that was so and said no more. They rode in companionable silence for a few miles. Tim's head was full of the events of last night and wondering if Josephine would be willing to share his bed again. Just the thought of her warm and welcoming body had his blood heating.

As the sun reached its height above them, they stopped to rest beside what Tim thought might be the Wingecarribee River. After watering the horses, they let the saddle horses graze, while Billy fed the wagon horses a small amount of grain. The lad had proved a useful helper—he said little and worked hard, especially caring for the horses. He had tossed a snake across the fire. Meanwhile Gilbert caught a large fish using the net Carlos fashioned, and was as excited as any boy catching his first fish.

Jo and Winnie decided they preferred fish to snake. Once they all finished eating, Jo wandered to the river to wash her hands and Tim followed her. Kneeling beside her, he asked, "How are you?"

She looked sideways at him and smiled. "I am well, thank you sir," was her reply. She then chuckled merrily. "We sound like a pair of nobs who are passing the time of day."

Tim joined in her laughter, and then said, "Carlos and Winnie are marrying at the first church or chapel we come across on our way. I expect she has told you."

She nodded. "Yes, isn't it grand? She is an admirable woman who has suffered at the hands of that awful brute who fathered her son, and Carlos seems like a kind person, so I wish them happiness, do you not?"

"Oh yes, but I fear they do not know each other well enough—after all, we have known each other for a far longer period and at times I fear I do not know you at all."

She touched the side of her neat nose and said with a smile, "Ah, but I have been told that it is best not to know each other too well, it is more interesting to learn things as you go along together."

"Another of your mother's wise teachings?"

"No, those wise words were from your Aunt Sara." She stood and wiped her hands down the side of her breeches and Tim did the same. "They had many ups and downs before finally finding the happiness they deserved."

Tim nodded, and then blurted, "I did not hurt you?"

She reached up and touched his face. "Of course not, I am hardier than I look, and not some weepy female who cringes at the least little touch." Leaning closer, she said softly, "I look forward to our times together getting better. Winnie assures me it does improve with practice." With a small laugh, she turned and sauntered back toward the others, now almost ready to move.

Tim sighed. There were times when he thought she was wise beyond her years, perhaps too wise, and now she had an older woman to offer her advice. In comparison, he was like a green lad, and feared she would always be too much for him to handle. Then again, he was certain she would offer him challenges he would relish. How was it he had thought her simply hotheaded for following him on this journey?

Bracken had run alongside the wagon all morning, so Tim lifted him up behind Jo as she took up the reins. His dog was besotted, and Tim fleetingly wondered what would happen if she decided to go her own way—which was likely.

Each day's riding had now become a routine, and little was said as the hours went by. They often caught sight of a mob of kangaroos, or a flock of birds overhead, but rarely saw other humans. A bullocky with his dray loaded with fleece had passed them on the road earlier, sparing a few minutes to stop and talk about the road ahead but it surprised Tim that they had seen no natives. He rode up beside Billy, and asked, "How do you plan to find any of your blood brothers, Billy, when we reach our destination? We have not spotted any of your kind at all. I fear they have all removed themselves far from the road and away from travellers."

The boy shrugged. "If it is meant to be then it will happen," he said. "I have been told there are more of my people down south where the white men have not yet had a chance to break up the tribes."

That was probably the most words he had spoken. "Is that why you decided to join Josephine on this journey?"

He shook his head. "I could do nothing else. I could not let her travel alone, and I had no wish to stay where I was, so this was the only thing to do." After a long silence, he said, "Her father made me promise to always stay by her side—until another comes along who would care for her."

"No doubt he knew how headstrong she is. The woman surely has a mind of her own, and I fear no man will ever be able to curb her appetite for adventure." Billy made no comment to that.

Towards the end of the afternoon, they arrived at Bong Bong, and Carlos dismounted to talk to a shepherd, questioning him on whether there was a minister in these parts. When he returned, he said to Tim, "We go on to Sutton Forest where we will find a chapel and also a minister." He rubbed his palms together. "The man said there is also a schoolhouse and the land hereabouts is owned by the nobs. He himself tends the sheep of one who has over 60 acres of rich pasture, granted by the Governor."

"I did learn that the Governor has a property in Sutton Forest called Hillview, where he can escape life in Sydney. Governor Macquarie himself commissioned the first survey through the area. It certainly is a beautiful part of the country, and Macquarie noted this when he visited over twenty years ago. Bong Bong was chosen as the government town, but it is said that Sutton Forrest has become the major stopping place for travellers."

"Then let us hope we can find decent lodgings." Carlos scratched his chin. "We shall see where Gilbert's thoughts lie then and hope he does not mind spending the night again with young Billy."

Tim was not about to answer that, for he still had his doubts about the boy. He seemed devoted to his mother, which in a way was odd, as most young men of his years would rather not spend so much time in the company of their mamas. Tim certainly did not—likely because he was sent off to Kings School at the age of twelve, so became well used to life away from his family.

Josephine pulled the horses to a halt just before they entered the village of Sutton Forest. She looked around and she and her companion laughed and clapped their hands. Presumably, they were excited at the sight of a weatherboard chapel set back a bit from the road. “And there is a schoolhouse alongside the chapel,” she called over a shoulder. “Shall we go there before finding an inn?”

Tim looked at Carlos, leaving it to him to decide, which he did, saying, “We go to the inn and the innkeeper will let us know if the minister is in residence.”

As he spoke, a man came out of the small cottage attached to the schoolhouse. He raised his hand in greeting shouting, “Welcome, travellers, do you need assistance?”

“We are after the minister.” Carlos nodded towards the chapel. “Is he in residence nearby or would we find him in the place of worship?”

The man came and leant on the small fence that surrounded both buildings. He looked to the sky. “At this time of the day you will doubtless find him inside. I did see him earlier, so you are lucky he is not off on his travels.” His hand encompassed the surrounding land. “He serves a wide parish.”

“Thank you, kind sir.” Carlos dismounted, and shook the man’s hand. “I will go and see if I can find him,” he said to Tim, before going through the small gate and over to the chapel doors.

Both women climbed down from the wagon and Jo came across to say, “Good day, sir, are you the teacher at this school?”

“Yes, I am Madam, and proud to be. The children come from all surrounding areas. Might I ask your final destination?”

“We hope to settle in Port Philip,” she said.

“And do you have any young ones or are you thinking of becoming a teacher when you reach the coast?”

She laughed, "Goodness me, no, I have no offspring yet and no husband even, but would like to perhaps be a teacher at some time in the future."

"Ah, then you will find you will be in need further south. I have heard that the children of some of the settlers run wild, free of a church or schoolhouse, and are becoming heathens."

"Goodness me, I am not sure I could cope with heathens," she said on a laugh.

Carlos strode across to them, looking pleased. "Come Winnie, the preacher wishes to speak with the bride." He took her arm and turned to Tim. "Would you and Jo come, too, he wishes to have a word with you also."

"With us, but why?" Tim put a hand on his chest as he frowned Jo's way.

Carlos shrugged, "Don't ask me, Tim lad, he is a man of the church and you know how odd some of them can be." As the four of them walked back to the door, he added, "We will need to stay over a day, as he cannot perform the ceremony until tomorrow."

The day was drawing to a close, and not a lot of light came in through the windows set high in the walls, so the chapel was dim and eerie. A tall man dressed in black breeches and jacket came towards them, a gaunt hand outstretched. "Welcome good folk, let us sit." He gestured to one of the rough-hewn pews, and once they were all seated, looked directly at Tim, and asked, "And what about you two, are you wishing to be wed as well?"

Tim shook his head with rather more vehemence than the simple question deserved, glancing sideways at Jo to gauge her reaction to the blunt question. In consternation, he saw her grinning his way. Tim cleared his throat, and said, "No, no, we are too young for marriage, sir."

That made the preacher chuckle. "Goodness me, lad, I have married some who are barely more than children. The rules seem to have changed since my young days back in Yorkshire."

Tim had no idea what to say to that. He stared at Jo, who was still finding this funny, which riled him somewhat. "Would you like to marry me?" he asked, in a moment of sheer idiocy, not for one moment expecting a sensible response from her.

When she said, "Well, I suppose we will wed one day, so why not now?" he ran a hand over his head and turned the hat he held around and around. This woman would see him completely mad before long.

The minister stopped him from finding a response by saying, "Well then, that is settled, come back here at ten thirty on the morrow and after my morning service I will marry you all." He pushed himself up, shook Carlos and Tim by the hand and ushered them from his church.

As they stood in the darkening evening Carlos thumped Tim on the back and said with a laugh, "So, lad, looks as if we are all to be wed."

Speechlessly Tim stared at Josephine who, if he sensed it correctly, seemed hesitant now the deed was done.

"Come, let us find a lodging before the sun sets completely," Carlos said, walking over to his horse. After helping Winnie onto the wagon, he mounted.

Tim did the same. They soon found a warm welcome at the inn, and luckily, Gilbert was happy to sleep beneath the stars again with Billy. They secured the horses in a small paddock behind the inn. Carlos seemed in a hurry to finish with eating, so it was that Tim and Josephine, plus Bracken, were alone in a room a mere hour or so later. She sat on the side of a bed and pulled off her boots.

"Are you quite certain about this marriage thing?" Tim asked, as he copied her and threw his boots one at a time to a corner.

"Are you not?" She chewed on the side of her bottom lip as she gave him a sidelong glance.

"Of course I am not. I thought it was usual for a suitor to declare his love for his chosen one and, apart from one jest back in Sydney, you have never expressed a desire to be married to me." Tim pulled his shirt over his head and tossed that onto the other bed, where Bracken had finished his turning ritual and was now gazing at them with his snout on his paws.

“Nor you to me. I think perhaps I was headstrong and caught up in the excitement of Carlos and Winnie being married.” She shrugged. “And perhaps it was the chapel and the minister. I imagine you did not mean it when you asked me if I was willing. What do we do? Should we tell the preacher we have changed our minds?”

Tim rubbed his hands over his face, then stared at her as she said, “Winnie tells me that I could already be with child. I had no idea that would happen after lying with you just the once. What do we do if that is the case?” Her lip took punishment again. “I do not believe her.”

That did not surprise Tim, for the same thought had already entered his mind. “Would you mind terribly… if you were to find you are carrying a baby—our baby?”

She knelt before him and placed her small hands on his chest. Tim shivered when she began to caress him and gently tug at the hairs there. “I think you would make an admirable father—you are a kind man, Timothy Carstairs. But I worry that you have no wish to be tied to one such as myself. I know my faults, and know they are many. For too long I have been allowed to do as I wish. I would hope that you would not try to curb my ways if I am your wife, for I fear I would not be dutiful.”

Tim grasped her fingers. Her gentle touch was preventing sensible thought. “Too true, Madam. I also worry, that you have ambition and an enthusiasm for life that might be curbed by being married.”

“That also is true, but who is to say what the future may bring? I am naïve in the ways of the gentry but know that many men take mistresses when they tire of their wife’s disinterest.”

“I have a feeling that I would take a long time to tire of you, Jo, and also believe that it is a husband’s duty to ensure that his wife does not grow disinterested in him.”

“Then let us wed.” She reached up and placed her palms on his cheeks. Tim pulled her close and kissed her. She melted and moved her hands behind his head. All sensible thought fled. There was no doubt that he would not soon tire of having her in his arms like this. Her mouth was as sweet as honey and her breasts against his chest made his heart beat faster. Eager to feel her naked flesh next to his own, he reached down and pulled her shirt up and over her head. Still impeded by some sort of chemise she wore he removed that, and then sighed his pleasure at the feel of her young body against his.

"Then let us wed," he repeated against her lips, as he stood and pulled her up with him. As he paused to take off his breeches, she did the same and removed all her clothing until they stood naked before each other. In that moment Tim was glad she was no shy maiden who might shrivel at his touch, instead a brave woman who offered herself so willingly to him. In the moment before he dragged her close, he muttered, "I do believe I am in love with you."

She stood on tiptoe and whispered, "And I you."

Tim lifted her to set her down on the bed and then came down beside her. Her skin was like the finest silk and he ran his fingers up and down her spine, loving the small shiver of what he felt sure was pleasure run over her skin. "You are fair to look at, my dear Josephine," he said as he bent to kiss each of her breasts until the points reached up to welcome him. "I fear I will hurt you."

"Never fear, I will set Bracken on you if you ever do," she said on a small laugh as he began to press small kisses from her chin to her stomach. When he reached the nest of hairs at her thighs she moaned softly and allowed him to do as he desired while she ran her fingers through his hair and uttered soft words of love.

When he could resist no longer and finally entered her warm body she sighed in contentment and Tim knew he would never find another woman who could bring him so much pleasure.

Chapter Eight

About ten townsfolk sat in the small chapel and Tim was glad there were people there to witness this momentous occasion. He and Carlos had donned the best breeches and shirts they could find amongst their sparse luggage. Josephine disappeared with Winnie soon after they all breakfasted, assuring him they would meet again at the chapel. Carlos rubbed his hands together and seemed nervous. "Are you still certain?" Tim asked.

"Yes, lad, I am more certain now, and what of you and your sweet lady, did either of you profess to doubts? After all it was most unexpected, was it not?"

"True. This time yesterday, I had not the slightest notion that by the end of this day I would be bound through marriage. But I am now certain it is the right thing to do. I am glad that my bride has Winnie to advise her."

"She is a wise woman, believe me Tim, and has been poorly treated. I pray that I will not disappoint her." He gave Tim a small nudge on the arm when the organist began to thump out a tune on his instrument.

The minister nodded and Tim turned towards the door. His eyes could only take in Josephine who was caught in a ray of sunshine that slanted across from one of the high windows. She wore a simple white gown and carried a small posy of wild flowers. There was a garland of flowers about her head and the uppermost thought in Tim's head was that he wished she had not cut her wonderful locks. He would ensure she never did such again. Their lovemaking could not be bettered, except he would welcome the time when her hair flowed to her waist in all its glory again so he could run his fingers through it. Bracken was at her side and he wagged his tail and grinned as he accompanied her down the centre walkway.

As she walked towards him, she smiled, and all around them disappeared. He knew not if Winnie walked beside or behind her. As she reached his side she whispered, "I am glad you have not run," and he wanted to laugh aloud at her audacity.

"And I am glad you decided to arrive." He picked up her hand and pressed a small kiss on the knuckle. Bracken flopped down near Tim's feet, but the minister seemed unbothered by the animal in his house of God.

If Tim was asked later the minister's words, in truth he would have to admit he heard but two words and that was his new bride saying, "I do," when asked if she wished to accept him in marriage. The rest went past in a blur. Once wed, they stepped to one side while the reverend repeated the service to Carlos and Winnie. Only then did Tim notice that she wore a deep blue gown of some plush fabric. The comparison between her and his fair Josephine was stunning.

After they signed the minister's book, and were walking up the aisle, Tim caught sight of Gilbert alongside Billy. Winnie's son did not look jubilant but more sullen than usual, while Billy's grin split his black face. Tim felt a moment's panic. He knew full well that blood would out and said again a silent prayer that the boy had not inherited any of his father's brutal ways, hoping that God in his wisdom heard his plea.

Nevertheless, he shrugged his doubts aside. Today was for celebration. Their small procession walked to the inn, where the innkeeper had kept his word and provided a fitting feast. Within an hour the four newly marrieds were merry, after quaffing ale, or in the ladies' case, wine. As soon as the meal was finished, Billy excused himself, saying he would tend to the horses. One of the animals that pulled the wagon needed a shoe replaced, and he had offered to take it to the blacksmith whose smithy was a short distance away. Gilbert followed him from the inn.

Tim was glad he had become attached to the native, trailing him everywhere.

Only a short time later Gilbert reappeared. As he stood by the door, Tim noted a man behind him. The boy was large, but whoever followed him seemed to tower over the lad. As if being shoved, Gilbert lurched forward, and it was then Tim realised that the man held a rifle aloft. He had a firm hold on the lad's arm. Winnie and Carlos had their backs to the door, but Jo gripped Tim's hand and whispered in a shaky voice, "That man is holding a weapon at Gilbert's back."

Tim nodded and at the same time, Winnie turned. Her scream of, "No," had Carlos on his feet. He was about to stride towards the intruder when Winnie grabbed his arm, and shouted again, "No!" then in a lower tone, "It is Gil's father, but how did he find us?"

"He must have followed her," Jo whispered.

The man pushed his captive forward and said in a guttural voice, "Thought you could take my son and run off, did ye, whore?"

In a moment of clarity, Tim noticed that Gilbert seemed unconcerned that the man, reported to be a brute, was holding him hostage with a rifle at his back. He also rapidly worked out that it was almost impossible for him to have arrived here in Sutton Forest on this day, unless he had been trailing Winnie and the boy from the moment she set out.

Sensing trouble, the other four diners, all men, hastily shuffled their way out through the door that led to the inner part of the inn. Bracken had been beneath the table gnawing happily on a bone provided by the cook but as Josephine rose and faced the intruder, saying, "There is no need to wave that rifle about. Tell us what you require," Bracken, hackles risen, pounced towards the man with a ferocious growl.

The man kicked out and caught the dog on the snout. With a yelp, Bracken stood his ground. At the same time Jo, fist raised, ran towards the man, screaming. He brought the hand that had been holding his son round and thumped her on the jaw. As his new wife fell to the ground, Tim rose and jumped towards her attacker, who then waved the rifle in front of him and pointed it at Jo, still lying dazed where she fell.

"Move another step and I shoot the wench," he growled. Carlos took a step forward but stopped when the man waved the rifle his way, snarling, "Stay where you are, I'm warning you all."

Ignoring him, Tim helped his wife up and sat her back onto her seat, where she slouched looking dazed. Bracken, hackles still raised, growled low, so Tim gave him a soft word of warning and he stepped back, but did not take his eyes from the brute. "What do you want?" Tim asked. "Tell us why you are here and be sensible about it. We do not want any more violence. What do you want with the boy? Let him go to his mother's side, I beg of you."

"Are you mad?" he had the audacity to accuse. "What I want is my wife, and my son, back where they belong."

Tim heard the gasp from Carlos, who stood with one arm about Winnie, who now sobbed, and the other hand clenched at his side. "Winnie is my wife, and was never yours, man." Tim had never heard such harshness from Carlos. "You are a fool to journey all this way for a woman who does not wish to be with a brute and a bully such as yourself."

"Fool am I?" He moved a step forward, but Carlos stood his ground. Winnie moved behind him. "Tis you who are the fool—this whore is mine and always will be, and her son wishes to be with his father. I will take both with me and be done with it, so stand back."

"You lie, Gabe, I was never your wife and you know it," Winnie said softly.

His laugh echoed about the room. "As good as," he roared. "Who bought you the fine clothes you wear and the baubles around your body?" He gestured towards her throat where the pendant she wore sparkled. "I treated you well and you know that much."

"You are a scoundrel and treated us both badly. We wish to be left alone. I would rather die than go back with you. And just as a matter of interest, how did you learn of our whereabouts?"

"Think me a fool, I say. I found out almost straight away where you were headed. All I had to do was hitch a ride on a trading ship heading south, and then jump ship on the coast and ride across country." His laugh said he was proud of himself. "I stole the horse from the first barn I came across and judged I would get here afore you, but no matter, I am here now, and you are coming with me."

"I am not going anywhere with you, and neither is Gil." Holding out a hand, she urged, "Come here son," but Gilbert did not move. He now looked confused and, even though now released, stood looking at his father. Then to Tim's astonishment he said clearly, "Go with Pa."

Tim looked across at Carlos, who appeared stunned. What had begun as a joyous day was now becoming a nightmare. "She does not wish to go anywhere but with me," Carlos said, shaking his head. "Take the boy and be gone."

"No," Winnie cried, as she took a step forward, and then rushed at Gilbert. She began to drag him away from his father, who now waved his weapon around as if he had no idea what to do with it. The loud sound of the rifle discharging was something Tim would carry with him always. Winnie slumped to the floor, blood staining the bodice of her gown.

Moaning, Carlos bent to tend to her, and then charged towards her assailant with a scream of rage. Fortunately, the man was so totally stunned by what he had just done, that Carlos was able to knock him to the ground and fling the rifle away from them. Holding the man down by the throat, he screamed abuse at him, while thumping him with his other fist until blood spurted from his lips.

Gilbert was now kneeling at his mother's side, making blubbering noises that resembled an animal in strife. Jo bent to help him up, but he refused her aid and shook her off. Tim put his finger to Winnie's neck but could feel no pulse. While all this had been going on someone must have had the sense to call the constable, as right then he stormed in, accompanied by a couple of other men and while one retrieved the rifle the other told Carlos he would now take care of Gabe.

Carlos went to stand above Winnie's lifeless body. Tears streamed down his face and dripped off his small beard. His bloody hands hung at his sides, and when Josephine went to put an arm about him, he ignored her.

The constable came across to Tim, while his two helpers dragged the murderer to his feet and pushed him out through the door. As he went, he shouted, "I just wanted what was mine. Why'd that fool of a woman have to go and do that?"

The constable nodded their way, saying, "We'll just ensure he is locked up. Don't anyone leave and we'll be back to question you. He will hang, be sure." He glanced down at poor Winnie and added, "The undertaker will be here soon."

Josephine came to Tim and gripped his hand. He could feel her tremble. "How is your face? I am so sorry—you should not have done what you did, foolish woman. I do not know what I would do if something happened to you." He touched her chin and when she winced at his soft touch, he muttered, "Sorry." Sitting on a chair, he pulled her onto his knee, and Bracken rested his nose on her knee while she stroked his head. "I hate to think of the pain Carlos is enduring." He nodded at his uncle, who now knelt by Winnie, head bent, shoulders shaking with his sobs. Gilbert sat opposite him, his arms about his knees and his head resting atop them as he rocked back and forth. "What of the lad now? He has no Ma and will have no Pa."

Jo's shoulders rose in a shrug. "I care not." Tim looked at her carefully. No doubt, still stunned by the events, it was unlike her to make such a comment. After a short break she whispered, "He was unafraid of his father, Tim. Could it all have been lies?"

"We will never know the truth now, unless the boy breaks his silence and begins to talk." Tim pulled her closer and rested his forehead on hers.

They sat, not saying any more, and after perhaps an hour, the minister came in and offered last rites. He appeared as stunned as they were and offered to stay until the undertaker arrived, which was another hour or so later. By the time Winnie's body was carried out, night was creeping in. The innkeeper asked what he could offer them in the way of refreshments but apart from Tim asking if Bracken, Billy and Gilbert could be fed, they refused food. As far as he knew, Gilbert also refused and when he disappeared outside, Tim presumed he went to help Billy with the horses.

Tim was hesitant to leave Carlos, but could see that Jo was exhausted so after ensuring his uncle was abed he went to her. After bathing her bruised and battered face, they lay silently in each other's arms for the remainder of the night. Tim barely slept, and knew she did not, as restlessly she tossed about, perhaps having another of her nightmares.

They laid Winnie to rest behind the chapel where only a day before, she wed Carlos. Tim was beginning to worry about his uncle, for barely a word passed his lips throughout the small ceremony and for an hour or more after they left the churchyard. Finally, Tim approached him and asked, "What would you have us do, Carlos? Do you wish to stay here longer, or shall we continue our journey?"

Carlos stared at him as if he did not quite understand him and then said, "Let us leave this place and be on our way."

Tim nodded and went to help Billy prepare the horses. The blacksmith had replaced shoes on both the shire horses and on Tim's mount. Gilbert was nowhere to be seen, and Billy admitted he had not slept aside him the night before. "What shall we do about the boy?" Tim asked Josephine.

"I fear he has gone off alone to grieve. Perhaps he wishes to be near his father. Should we tell the constable he is missing, do you think?" Tim agreed, so that is what they did. The constable assured them that he would keep his eyes open but also said that the boy was old enough to fend for himself and so was not his responsibility. Carlos seemed not to care where the lad was or what he was doing.

When they left the town behind, the sun was almost above them. Tim decided they would keep going until they came across another inn or likely place to camp for the night. About twelve miles from Sutton Forest, Billy said, "The boy Gilbert has been following us. When we stop he stops."

With a hand up to shield her eyes from the sun, Jo looked back the way they had come. "I cannot see him. Perhaps he will join us when night falls. If so, we must offer him refuge, for the poor boy has no one now to care for him."

Tim was not about to argue with his new wife, but had the thought that Gilbert was no boy, but a man who must now fend for himself.

Night was almost upon them when they reached the small village of Murrimba aside Saint Patrick's Creek. Thankfully, there was accommodation at the newly opened Jolly Millar Inn. The owner introduced himself as Willoughby Beadman when he welcomed them. The pastures were lush, and so the horses had good grazing. They left Billy in charge of the animals. After they had eaten their meal, Tim went out to check that Billy fared all right.

No rain was expected and if the weather should change, he had the wagon for shelter. Bracken followed him and went off to cock his leg up a river gum. When he began to growl, Billy said, "Gilbert is yonder."

"Come here, lad." At Tim's call, Gilbert slid out from his hiding place. Bracken still growled, so Tim quietened him, and then said, "You must be hungry, boy. Come out. The dog will not harm you." When Gilbert slowly came over, Tim noted he looked bedraggled and weary. "Come with me, and I will ask the cook if he can find you something to fill your belly."

Feet dragging along the ground, Gilbert followed him. They had travelled at a faster pace than usual this day, mainly because Carlos seemed intent on putting distance between himself and the place where he had lost Winnie, so the lad must have run full pelt to keep apace with them.

Once he had eaten, he went outside—Tim guessed to sleep aside Billy. He said naught the whole time, and Tim wondered if words would now ever come out of his mouth. When he joined Jo in their room, where she already lay beneath the coverlet, he said as much.

"If he travels with us, I will try to teach him the letters and perchance he will then start to speak. I think the words he uttered were more through shock than anything else—perhaps in time we can shock him out of his silence. There is hot water there if you wish to bathe. I asked the maid to fetch more."

Tim knelt on the side of the bed and bent to kiss her. "Thank you, my love. You smell as sweet as meadow flowers, and I must stink like a pig who has frolicked in mud."

After stripping off his clothes, Tim poured water into the bowl. As he began to rub soap onto his chest, she came up behind him and took it from his hand, whispering, "Let me, husband."

"With pleasure." He passed the cloth to her and she did an excellent job of washing the grime from his body. When he could stand her gentle ministrations no longer, he muttered, "Let us be rid of this," as he bent to pull her gown up and over her head. Bracken thought they played a game and wanted to join in the fun, so Tim gave him a soft order to go to his bed, a blanket she had set for him in a corner. The dog obeyed and did his usual turns before settling down with a contented grunt.

"Where were we?" Tim took her hand and led her back to the bed where he pushed her gently back and came down beside her. "Have I told you how much your body pleases me?" he asked as he stroked his fingers across one breast and then the other. Her soft shudder told him his touch pleased her.

"No, but you can tell me now," she whispered against his chest as she pressed her body against his in a sensuous movement.

"I love this." He pressed a kiss to one breast. "And this." He did the same to the other and then every part of her luscious sweet body, until she was crying out for him to be inside her.

He did not keep her waiting. As they lay in the aftermath of their fiery mating, Tim wondered if perhaps the tragedy that befell Carlos made each of them more aware of how precious life was. Now he knew what it was like to share love, he was afraid. It had taken him a while to realise he loved this woman beside him, and knowing such love made him aware of what pain he would suffer if he lost her.

Chapter Nine

When they neared the Murumbidgee River, they were on the thirteenth day of their journey. The new township of Gundagai sat by the river. Along the way, a traveller going towards Sydney Town had warned them that bushrangers were about in the area, and they should be on their guard.

"I do hope we find a decent inn to place our heads down this night," Jo said.

Tim feared she was tiring of the journey and had to admit he was also feeling the strain of the long silences from Carlos, who seemed to have lost interest in life itself since Winnie's death.

After leaving Murrimba, they headed for Goulburn, so named after Henry Goulburn, who at that time was the Under-Secretary of State for War and the Colonies. They passed over the Goulburn Plains. The land about was originally settled by landowners who appreciated what Governor Macquarie had called, 'a most beautiful rich tract of land, with grass so high the cattle stood up to their bellies in the lush sweet meadowland'. The produce of the area had kept Sydney in food during a drought that hit the settlers hard in 1838. The town boasted a recently opened inn, The Coach and Horses, a brewery, and a hospital built primarily for the convicts who constructed the road south from Picton. A nearby stockade accommodated these convicts, and unfortunately, a flogging post and gallows were stark reminders to the travellers that escaped convicts were an ever-present danger on the road south.

Next, they passed over the Breadalbane Plains, and then climbed the Cullarin Range, dubbed The Razorback by the bullock drivers who hated it. Hamilton Hume had been allocated over a thousand acres in the area to honour his exploration achievements. After experiencing the trials of a long trek overland, Tim was more in awe of such accomplishments by men like Hume who set out with merely an estimate of where they were heading.

At Yass, Tim sent his final messages back to the Government in Sydney Town, and to his Mama and Pa and Uncle Remy, assuring them they were all safe. He did not mention the tragedy that had befallen Carlos, deeming it up to his uncle to relay his misfortune, if he so wished. He wondered what his Ma would think of him now being a married man. She had always encouraged him to think with his heart, so was sure she would be overjoyed at his choice of bride.

The rich and fertile land of the Yass Valley belonged to the Ngunnawal people. When Tim asked Billy if he wished to seek them out, he was reluctant. There was still unrest between the natives and the settlers. They also heard that bushrangers had caused such havoc in the area that a jail and courthouse were built in Yass in 1835. Tim often wondered if Billy would ever find people of his tribe in this vast land.

Once they left Yass behind, Tim knew the road would become harsher, with less inns, and they still had about four hundred miles to traverse. They met a man who warned them, as others had, that some of the squatters were no better than ruffians and blaggards in these parts. Likely because there were no preachers, no schools and no Post Office.

On nearing Gundagai, a settler eyed Billy warily saying, "His people favour this land hereabouts." He gestured everywhere. "The Wiradjuri's seem to like living alongside the river with its red river gums offering shelter." He scratched his head and added, "Mind you, they also warn us whites that we should be careful—they seem to know when the river is about to flood." With a shudder he said, "Give me the creeps they do." Tim made no comment to that. His opinion of Billy was high—the lad never shirked and was devoted to Jo.

His opinion of Gilbert differed. The lad also seemed devoted to her but in a different way—a way that was beginning to make Tim uneasy, and he was not sure just why. When he broached this subject with her, she said, "I think he has transferred his adoration of his mother to me. He is doing well with his letters and can spell a few simple words. He is willing to learn. I feel sorry for the boy. I know what it is like to lose your parents under horrific circumstances."

Tim could well understand that, but nonetheless was jealous of the time she spent with Gilbert, time that could be better spent with him. After a days' travelling all Tim wished to do was be alone with her in the privacy of their room or tent when they retired for the night. He still wasn't reconciled with the fact that Gilbert had not appeared scared of his father—a fact that would likely always puzzle Tim, who found it difficult to gauge the lad's feelings.

Carlos ignored Gilbert and barely looked his way. After the boy caught up with them, they had found a change of clothing for him in the bag left behind by Winnie. They also found more jewelry but did not disclose this to him. Carlos stashed it away, along with the baubles she was wearing when killed. When Tim questioned him on this Carlos said, "There is little point leaving it for the undertaker to steal. Perhaps it will fetch a good price should I ever need it."

Tim felt a section of his uncle's heart had closed off, making him bereft of feeling. "Time will heal him," was Jo's response when he said as much to her. All they could do was hope that some day he would return to his former self.

As yet, there was no inn in the newly formed township of Gundagai, so after crossing the river at its lowest point, they made camp along its banks. Night was falling when they finished their meal. Jo detested eating kangaroo meat, but after so many days on the road, there were times when they were forced to kill an animal for food. After rinsing the cooking pot, she came towards the fire and stopped in her tracks.

Tim followed her gaze and reached for his rifle. At least ten native men stood beyond the light of their fire, so black they almost melded into the night. When he hailed them, they didn't move or respond. Billy had been ensuring the horses were tethered to the rope he had set up, enabling them to graze on the lush riverside grass. Coming over to Tim, he placed a hand on the rifle, saying, "I will speak to them."

Gilbert was closer to the group of men, and when Billy gestured to him, the lad went down on his haunches. Billy neared the closest native and spoke so softly that Tim failed to hear what was said. Jo put down the pot and came to stand beside Tim and Carlos, who had also left what he was doing to stare at the group. Naked except for a small scrap of what looked like animal hide covering their genitals, they all carried long spears. Their hair reached their shoulders in matted clumps, adding to their frightening appearance.

When the one Billy spoke to waved his spear Tim took a couple of steps forward, but Jo caught him by the arm and whispered, "Leave Billy to do this alone."

"What is it you want?" Carlos shouted and the one waving the spear then pointed it towards him.

Billy turned and came back. When he said, "I can go with them," Jo gasped.

Clearly worried, she asked, "Do you wish to?"

"Their camp is not far. I will spend the night with them and perhaps stay. I do not understand all they say, but they know a few of the white man's words." Billy rubbed his hands together and Tim could not decipher if he was excited or worried.

"Go Billy, and if you do not return by the morning when we are ready to travel, we will come looking for you. I would wish to know that you fare well." Tim patted him on the shoulder and Billy nodded, before walking back towards the group.

Gilbert mumbled something before following him. Two of the men shouted in their native tongue, waving their spears and fists, and Gilbert faltered, and then stopped. He went down on one knee, his head bent, as Billy walked off with them. Soon, the night swallowed them up, and it was as if they had never been there.

"Do you think he will be safe?" Jo asked. Tim shook his head, not knowing the answer.

Carlos shrugged. "It is why the black fella came along with us, is it not?" Tim said nothing and neither did Jo as she turned away and continued with her task of clearing up.

Soon they were in their tent and as Tim pulled her close, she whispered, "I am certain they would not kill one of their own kind, would they?"

"Carlos had the truth of it. Billy sought his own people, and if he has found them, then we must be happy for him. If he is in danger, then we will help him. I do not fear for his life." Tim's kiss could not soothe her fears, and they spent another restless night.

When they rose, the sun was barely up, doing nothing to dispel the chill in the air. The grass was heavy with morning dew, and Carlos already had the fire going. As he tossed a stick on it, he said, "The idiot boy has gone. The fool must have trailed Billy."

Jo put a hand to her mouth, crying, "No! He would get lost away from the road." There were many river gum trees in the area, and it was a fact that once away from the river a man could easily disappear into the shrubs and undergrowth. "We must go after him. I see Billy has not returned either." Clearly agitated, she began to throw things into the bag she used overnight.

"I for one will not risk my life for them. Billy chooses to be with his kind, and I owe the boy Gilbert nothing. He has done little to prove himself and is nothing more than a nuisance." Carlos spat into the fire and turned to continue packing his tent.

"You have become very hard hearted," Jo called after him. Tim agreed with her—the old Carlos would never have shown such callousness towards another human.

"Life has done little for me to make me any other way." Carlos began to toss things into the wagon.

"You are not the first person in this world to lose someone you love," she shouted, but Carlos ignored that.

"Leave him." Tim put a hand on her arm. "He will soon be back to his old self once his grieving is done with."

"I hope so," she muttered. "We must find Billy, if not Gilbert." Her eyes filled with tears and Tim pulled her close. "I will not go on until I know he is safe."

Carlos was now saddling the horses. He had secured Billy's mount and the packhorse behind the wagon, where the shires were already harnessed. "We will seek Billy and see if we can find Gilbert," Tim called. "You can stay and ensure our belongings are safe, Carlos. If we do not return in an hour or so, then find the constable, if there is one in town, and inform him of our whereabouts."

As Tim and Jo mounted their horses, Carlos muttered a few curses, and shook his head. "You are a fool to waste time on them, but if that is what you wish to do, then so be it. I will guard everything well and give you until the sun is nearly at its height. If you are not back by noon, I will take the wagon and horses into town."

When they had only ridden a short distance away from the camp, Tim began to think that they were likely on a foolish errand. "Stay close," he said, and Jo nodded. Bracken trailed them, tail wagging, sensing this was some sort of game. Once the sun was up, sweat soon poured down his back. "We must keep the river in sight, or we will easily lose our way."

Away from the road and the river, the surrounding countryside looked the same wherever they were. A man could easily get lost out here and his body never found. The shrill song of a thousand birds filled the air, and many coloured parrots flew about, anxious at having their habitat invaded. They fascinated Jo. She still took out her notebook as often as she was able, and it was now filled with the many creatures she had drawn along the way.

After half an hour or so, Tim said, "I've lost any signs of people passing this way. Perhaps we should call and see if we get an answer." He feared Carlos was right and this was the stupidest thing they could have done, but his wife was intent on ensuring her friend was safe so he said nothing. They began to call out Billy's name, but the only sound that returned to them was from the birds, upset by this human intrusion.

When they stopped to listen, she said, "Surely they cannot be further away." She took off her hat and wiped the sweat from her face on her neckerchief.

"It's a fact that the natives travel vast distances. They know the land well. I do not think we should venture further, Jo. To get lost in this place is to die. We are not skilled as the natives are." The words were barely out of Tim's mouth when the sound of several gunshots filled the air. The noise upset the parrots, who flew off in a frenzy of squawking. Bracken began to bark, his ears pricked as he stared back the way they had come, his tail held high.

"That comes from behind us." Tim wheeled his horse. "We must go back, love."

"No, I will not desert Billy." That stubborn glint shone in her eye. "That is more than likely hunters shooting at kangaroos."

"It is not you who desert him. He chose to go, and as for Gilbert, I agree with Carlos, the boy is old enough to take care of himself and chose to follow Billy." Another round of gunshots rang through the air. "That is never hunters—they would not be so wasteful with their shots. Come, we will go back and then decide what to do next." When she still looked hesitant, he urged, "Please."

It was clear she wanted to argue further, but when more shots rang through the air, and Tim kicked his horse into a canter, she followed. As they neared their camp, shouting was added to the gunshots. Tim slowed his mount, gesturing for Jo to keep behind him. As Bracken darted forward, he ordered, "Keep back."

The scene before them was one of chaos. Four men of disreputable appearance stood around, all pointing their rifles towards the sky. The contents of the wagon lay strewn across the grass. Carlos, his hands bound, sat in front of a large tree. Tim hissed, "Quiet," when Bracken barked, but his warning came too late.

One of the bushrangers caught sight of them and turned his rifle in their direction, shouting, “Well, well, what do we have here?”

“We have nothing of value.” Tim dismounted, catching Carlos’s shake of the head in warning. “We are just travellers and carry nothing but the clothes we wear.” Gesturing at the mess they had made, he added, “As you have no doubt found for yourselves.”

The man seemed to lose interest in Tim, and walked towards Jo, who now stood beside her horse. “And what is a pretty little bundle like this doing travelling along with you fellas?” Stepping close to her, he reached out to touch her face, and as she cringed away from him, Tim took the opportunity to thump him across the head. He fell at Tim’s feet and Tim grabbed his rifle and pulled Jo clear. Pushing her behind him, he aimed the rifle at the man’s head. Bracken now pounced and, hackles raised, grabbed a mouthful of the man’s shirtsleeve and shook it as he growled fiercely.

Reaching out with his free arm, the man punched Bracken, who yelped but refused to let go. “Do not harm my dog or you will die now,” Tim snarled, “Get up and get on your way.” He waved the rifle at the other three bandits who now had their weapons aimed at him.

“We’ll kill yer,” shouted one, while another moved closer still.

Tim fired the rifle at his feet, and he jumped back, the look of surprise on his face comical if Tim was in the mood for a laugh. Tim prayed that he would not run out of shots. “We do not wish for bloodshed any more than I guess you do. Now what I suggest is that you get on your way and leave us in peace.” It was obvious that these men were not skilled in the ways of bushrangers. Had they been bloodthirsty types, Carlos would doubtless be dead or unconscious.

The one lying on the ground was still pounding at Bracken who refused to let go of his quarry. Tim was about to kick him in the back when Jo bashed the man over the head with a thick branch she had picked up. “That’s for harming our dog," she screamed as he fell back. She then grabbed Bracken by the collar and pulled him away. So occupied was Tim with watching her in surprise that he failed to notice one of the other three thugs moving closer.

"Watch out, Tim," Carlos yelled, just in time, and Tim brought the rifle up and whacked him on the chin with the end of it. Dropping his weapon, the man stumbled back.

A blood-curdling scream echoed through the trees and Gilbert ran out of the shadows and threw himself at the other two thugs who had been watching as if they had no idea what to do next. Grabbing each by the neck, he bashed their skulls together with such force, Tim felt sure he must have broken their necks. They both slumped to the ground as the one Tim had hit stood groggily, shaking his head. When Gilbert grabbed him by the scruff and punched him square on the jaw, he too tumbled to the ground like a rag doll.

The one lying near Tim began to scramble to his feet, and Gilbert halted his progress by kicking him in the back. His face split in a grin as he turned to Tim and said clearly, "Are my friends hurt?"

Jo gaped at him in surprise, and asked, "Where's Billy?" He shook his head, turned back and went to pick up all the rifles lying on the ground. After placing them onto the wagon, he then walked off through the trees.

Tim went over and cut through the rope binding Carlos, asking, "What now?"

Carlos looked at the four on the ground, as he rubbed at his wrists. "I'm sorry, Tim lad, I didn't hear them approach. They caught me by surprise."

Still stunned by the events, Tim patted him on the shoulder. "Not to worry, as long as you are all right."

Carlos walked to the one nearest Tim and, pushing the man back, thrust his hand into the pocket of his filthy breeches. Grinning, he held a bunch of banknotes aloft, saying, "I believe this is ours." He then cuffed him across the head. Going over to one of the other no-gooders, he pulled Winnie's jewels from his pocket.

Gilbert reappeared, leading two horses the thieves had obviously secreted a distance away. "We keep these?" he asked. Billy followed him, leading another two.

Jo ran to him, crying, "You came back. Did you not wish to stay with your kinfolk, Billy?"

Billy shook his shaggy head. "No, missus, they were not of my blood—but they told me that I will find more tribes as we near our destination, and perhaps I will meet them there."

Bracken growled at the man he had been guarding as he began to move, rubbing at his head. Tim went to stand over him. "We have no need for more horses, but I do not wish to leave them here for this lot." He kicked the man's leg. "Unsaddle them and let them roam free. These rogues can seek refuge in the town if they so wish but until they capture their horses, they will not be able to terrorise more travellers. Leave the saddles. We keep their rifles."

As they left the four men, all shouting abuse after them, Tim said, "We will inform the constable, if there is one in town, and he can do as he sees fit with them, but in future we each have a weapon handy. I fear we may come up against more like them—and perhaps worse types, before we reach our destination. You do know how to handle a rifle, do you not, Jo?"

"Of course I do." She still appeared stunned by the episode and kept glancing over her shoulder.

There was no constable available so, eager to put as much space as possible between them and the thieves, Tim said, "I would prefer not to camp out this night, so I think we should continue until we find an inn of sorts."

Both Carlos and Jo agreed. Tim rode alongside Jo and said softly, "Your gold is safe?"

She nodded. He still had no idea where she had it concealed, but she must have hidden it well. He knew that, thankfully, she kept her money in a belt around her middle, as he did. Lord knows how they would fare if all was lost. Tim recalled how his Uncle Remy buried his gold somewhere in the hills and collected it when passing back through the mountains to Bathurst. He shuddered as he remembered Remy's terrifying story of his capture by bushrangers who forced him to accompany them on a robbery. Had the thieves today been a more bloodthirsty or experienced gang, it could have ended in disaster for them all.

Riding alongside Carlos, he said, "I did not know you had cash concealed in the wagon."

Carlos smiled for the first time since the tragedy. "It is the property of Gilbert now, I think. It was in with Winnie's few possessions. She had more than she claimed. If the boy needs it at a later date, it will be his."

Around noon, they reached an inn they learned was opened by the owner of a large acreage called Tumbalong. The innkeeper stressed how lucky they were that it was a fine day, as on some days the nearby Adelong Creek crossing place proved a hazard for travellers.

After a meal, and resting the horses, they continued on as Tim hoped to reach the next village before nightfall. The innkeeper, a talkative sort, assured him that one Thomas Mate recently added an inn and store to his homestead in the village that was about halfway between Sydney Town and their destination.

The creek reached the top of the wagon wheels, but Jo managed the crossing well, filling Tim with admiration. His new wife seemed to manage every obstacle thrown her way. The incident with the bushrangers would have sent some women screaming to the nearest place of sanctuary, but she seemed determined not to let it distress her. "You are not tiring?" he asked once they were on the other side.

The road at times was now little more than ruts left by travellers gone before them, which made it hazardous. Often, she had to negotiate around many large holes and bumps. When she said, "I am fine," Tim had his doubts, sure her slender frame was not made for driving a wagon over many miles, but her stubbornness would never allow her to admit as such.

"Would you prefer to ride for a while? I could take over the wagon—or perhaps Gilbert can now that we have learned he is to be trusted."

She shook her head. “Perhaps tomorrow.” There was no doubt that her spirits had lowered since losing Winnie. Last night as they lay in bed, she wept again for the woman so cruelly slain, saying between her tears, “I can well understand Carlos’ grief. She was wise in many ways, reminding me of Matilda, my teacher and companion.”

Night had fallen when they arrived at the inn. After the longest trek so far, they were all travel weary, so were soon in their beds. Jo fell asleep as soon as she lay down. Tim watched her, his head whirling with thoughts. Should he have started out on this venture? They were only halfway, yet it seemed as if they had been on the road endlessly. Carlos was looking haggard, and Tim guessed he, too, must look worn. Perhaps if Winnie had not been so cruelly killed, they would all be feeling more cheerful. What started out as a grand adventure was turning into a trial of endurance.

If the bushrangers had not attacked them, he might be feeling differently but as it was, he now fretted daily, worrying they might be attacked again along the road as it became less populated. His worry was not for himself but for the brave woman who slept soundly by his side. If not for his foolish thirst for adventure they would still be in Sydney—but then again it was doubtful if she would now be his wife if that were the case.

Perhaps this was Fate’s way of determining they be together.

Chapter Ten

"Soon we will cross what is called The Murray River." Tim gestured ahead. The last few days had been hazardous and wearisome for them all. After leaving the village after Gundagai, they crossed numerous creeks, some flooded. Gilbert was happy to take over the driving of the wagon while Jo sat alongside him. He still talked little, but Jo managed to hold a conversation of sorts with him. She was steadily teaching him his letters—Tim guessed it helped pass the endless hours of watching the rumps of the horses as they plodded along before them.

Tim's log told him that they left Sydney eighteen days ago. One thing that heartened him was that the town alongside the river, now known as Albury, possessed a barracks. Soldiers, dubbed the Border Police, were established in the area, perhaps to catch bushrangers, runaway convicts, or more likely to repress the natives. It gave a sense of security, knowing any thieves roaming the area would be more cautious now.

Countless men women and children of the Wiradjuri tribes were massacred in an uprising nine years ago but, from what he learned, the natives had since settled down. Tim turned to Billy, saying, "Perhaps you might find your people here."

Billy shrugged. "It might be I will never find my own clan. I was taken from them so many years ago, and everything has changed—so many were slain." The boy seemed to accept his fate without question, which surprised Tim. Or, perhaps because he spent so many years with white folk, he was now unsure exactly where he belonged in society.

Rain had fallen steadily since just after noon and apart from feeling weary, they all looked forlorn and bedraggled. A passing bullocky told them that an inn had opened in this small settlement only last year, so they would have a chance to dry out. Billy and Gilbert were quite happy to weather any storm, as against sleeping beneath a solid roof. Thankfully, the wagon afforded them shelter from the worst of the weather.

The inn sat apart from the police barracks, a blacksmith's shop, and a scattering of houses. Once they dined, they were not long from their beds. The rain continued throughout the night, to Tim's dismay, for the innkeeper assured them that the river could run fast after such a downpour. In the morning as they were preparing to set off, he said, "You would be wise to tread carefully. The crossing place has been chosen well, but there are times when the river can be deep in places."

"We were told such about the Adelong crossing, but managed that with little problem. But I thank you for your warning. We will take care, be sure." Tim saluted and went to mount his horse.

Jo looked apprehensive when they reached the place to cross, asking, "Should we wait a day?" After encountering numerous creeks along the way, she was well used to the wagon getting stuck, but this one certainly looked more menacing, and was running fast. So far, they had managed to get out of trouble, and Gilbert's strength proved an asset.

Tim turned to Carlos asking the same question, but Carlos' shrug said he cared little. Tim had begun to wonder if he would ever snap out of this melancholy mood and return to his former cheerfulness. After a pause, when he studied the water, Tim finally said, "It might get worse, so I suggest we leave now. I have no desire to dally here waiting for it to drop."

The black as night water looked forbidding. Two travellers went before them, and when they reached the middle, the water swirled around the top of their wagon's wheels. Tim looked to Gilbert, saying, "Carlos and I will follow the path they have taken, so you stay close to us."

Gilbert nodded. As Tim urged his horse forward, he heard the reins slapping on the horses' rumps. He was grateful that their mounts were undaunted by the water, and by now the two hitched behind the wagon also took all in their stride.

The other travellers were climbing up the opposite bank when Tim and Carlos reached mid-river, their horses' heads held high. Just about to say that they had done well so far, a shout from behind them was followed by a splash and then another. As Tim pulled his horse up, he looked over a shoulder. Bracken was in the water, battling against the strong current, but worse, Jo was not on the bench beside Gilbert, who was now standing, shouting and waving his arms above his head. All this startled the shires who began to move forward. He managed to grab the reins, and they stopped.

This all happened so fast that by the time Tim looked around to ensure Bracken was safe, both dog and Jo were a good few feet downriver. She was shouting something he could not make out above the pounding of his heart. Tossing his reins to Carlos, Tim jumped from his horse. The water came up to his chest, but as he neared Jo it got deeper, which meant he had to swim, not the easiest with his clothing dragging him down.

Bracken changed direction and began heading to the opposite bank, but Jo's arms were still flailing about. She looked to be panic-stricken, and Tim could not understand what she was screaming at him. Fear, such as he had never known, gave strength to his arms and as he got closer to her, he could tell that she was floundering.

"Can you swim?" he yelled, but she continued to scream words he could not make out. Then her head disappeared beneath the water and Tim's heart thumped like a drumbeat inside his chest. "Jo," he screamed.

As he reached the spot where she sank beneath the water, she reappeared long enough for him to grab her by the arm. With difficulty, he trod water as he pulled her against him and lifted her high. After a few coughs and splutters, she gasped his name, and then cried, "Bracken?"

In his distress, Tim had forgotten about his dog. There had been no choice about which of them to save. "He is a good swimmer," he said, hoping that was the truth, as he began to swim awkwardly towards where he thought the water was shallower. Carlos had reached the other bank and as Tim neared him, he came and took Jo from his arms, carrying her to the bank.

"Did Bracken get across?" Tim asked as he waded to dry land and took Jo from Carlos.

Carlos shook his head. "I was looking at you and not the dog," he said, as he glanced about.

Jo began to sob. "It was my fault," she moaned. "He slid off the bench and I couldn't reach him."

Tim kissed her wet cheek. "Don't blame yourself. You are shivering—let us get you out of these wet clothes." The rain had ceased, but there was still a chill in the air.

Gilbert stood a short distance up the bank, moving from foot to foot in his distress. He had moved the wagon well away from the river, and all the horses were busily pulling at the long grass beneath their hooves. The native was not with them. Jo looked about and cried, "Where's Billy?" When Gilbert pointed along the riverbank, Tim could see nothing there. More intent on getting Jo out of her wet clothing, he hurried to the wagon.

Billy still had not returned by the time they were all in dry clothing. Jo paced back and forth calling the native's name. The fire they lit to dry off their clothing blazed merrily, and a weak sun now peeped through the clouds, when she shouted, "Bracken," and began to run along the riverbank.

The dog came to her, wagging his tail and she dropped to put her arms about him, sobbing into his wet fur. A short time later Billy strolled towards them. Tim shook his hand and patted him on the back, saying, "Thank you."

"I met some black fellas along there." Billy gestured over a shoulder. "They saw the dog in trouble and helped him. They like animals," he added, and then walked to his horse, stroking his hands over it, before going to the others to ensure they suffered no ill effects.

Tim went to his side, asking, "Did you not wish to spend time with them, Billy?"

He shrugged, said, "No," and carried on with his task.

Tim bent to pat Bracken, who planted wet kisses on his cheek as he wagged his tail fit to drop off. Returning to the fire, where Carlos was boiling the billycan, he said, "We will rest a while before we go on." Putting an arm about Jo's shoulders, he chided, "Do not ever scare me like that again." He sensed her shivers were more to do with worry than with the cold.

"I was foolish." She shook her head. "I should have realised that Bracken could swim better than I."

* * *

Because they had spent more time than anticipated at Albury, it was three days later when they reached the Ovens Crossing Place, as Sir Thomas Mitchell had named it not long ago. As they neared the river, Tim said to Carlos, "I pray this river is not also flooded. I know there is a punt established now so I can ensure Jo gets over safely." She had a nightmare the night after her ordeal, causing Tim another sleepless night. "There is also an inn on the south side of the river."

After Albury, they passed no inns. Tim knew Jo tired of sleeping in the tent. In fact, he felt she tired of travelling altogether, and admitted privately he wished he had not started on this venture—cursing his wish for a more exciting life.

He estimated they should now reach their destination in five or six days. When he said as much to her last night, she said nothing. "I did tell you it would take perhaps a month, did I not?" he reminded her.

"That you did. I still do not regret following you." She glanced at him. Their tent was dim—lit only by the one small lamp, but he sensed rather than saw her uncertainty when she added, "Are you sorry I joined you, Tim? Perhaps you now wish you had not wed this stupid female."

“You are not stupid, and I have no regrets, although I do at times wish we had wed under different circumstances.” Tim pulled her close. “Kiss me, my sweet, and promise me you will learn to swim before we finish this journey.” There was no time for more words as they came together.

Luck was on their side and the horses were all able to get safely across the river. Gilbert was now proving expert at driving the wagon. Jo willingly crossed on the punt, Bracken at her side. Gilbert still spoke little, but Jo persevered with him, which Tim thought commendable. One thing that still niggled though was that he often caught Gilbert looking at Jo with more than friendship and gratitude in his gaze.

After they’d eaten, Tim and Jo retired to their room, leaving Carlos still drinking with one of the other customers, a rough looking cove who was travelling northwards with a bullock team. As he stripped, preparing to bathe, Tim voiced his fears. “Has Gilbert ever done anything unseemly?” he asked. “I fear he has other thoughts beside friendship in mind.”

Jo took the cloth from him and began to wash his chest, saying, “Rubbish. I think he is grateful that we allowed him to travel with us, after what went before.”

“It’s not gratitude I see in him, but something more.” Tim kissed her on the nose. “You will let me know, will you not, should he do or say anything that you find offensive? He is large and I would not wish to have to confront him.”

She laughed as she continued to bathe his upper body. “I have a feeling, husband dear, that you would have the best of it, despite the fact that you are so puny and he is so huge.”

“Tis puny, am I?” Grabbing the cloth from her, he began to tickle her in all the places he now knew were sensitive to his touch. They fell back onto the bed, laughing and kissing.

“You know you are not,” she whispered, as he pulled her shirt over her head and tossed it and then her undergarment aside. "You are all that I would wish in a man."

Tim awoke with a start some hours later. A string of curses followed a loud crash from the room adjoining theirs. "Carlos," Tim said on a sigh as Jo stirred. She rolled over and huffed but did not wake. Rising with stealth, he pulled on his breeches—opened the door, and went to knock softly on his uncle's door.

Carlos mumbled a few indistinct words, so Tim went inside. Carlos lay on the floor curled in a heap. He cursed again as he tried unsuccessfully to rise. "What you want?" he grumbled, peering up at Tim.

"I wondered what all the noise was about. Are you all right? Why are you lying down there?"

"Because I like lying on the boards, why the bloody hell do you think I am down here?" he shouted, once again trying to get up. Tim gave him a helping hand, and managed to get him onto his bed, where Carlos flopped back, a hand over his face. "I should have stayed in bloody Bathurst," he grumbled.

"Nonsense. We are all feeling a bit fed up with this journey, but once we reach our destination all will be well, you'll see."

"No, it won't. It will never be right again for me—do you not see?" Carlos sat up and put his feet to the floor, and then sat hunched, palms over his face as he rocked back and forth. "I loved her. I know you felt it was too rushed and perhaps she was not right for me, but Winnie loved me." His whine finished on a loud hiccup.

"I know." Tim pushed him back down onto the bed again and took off his boots. He had never seen his uncle so drunk or disconsolate before. "But someone else will come along, you'll see, and you will find love again."

Tim doubted he was heard, as Carlos was now snoring loudly. Tim pulled his breeches off, covered him with the blanket, and left him to his drunken dreams. Perhaps it was true love between him and Winnie, they would never know. Tim sighed as he crept out and closed the door behind him.

Jo was awake when he returned to their bed. "Is he all right?" she asked softly as she put her arms about him.

"Just the worse for drink and feeling sorry for himself."

"How strange life is," she said. "If not for Winnie and Carlos wishing to be wed it could be that we would not have married on that fateful day."

He echoed her feelings but did not respond. One thing was certain, when he held her in his arms, and she melted beneath his touch, Tim cared not if they were wed or not. When he awoke as the day broke, Jo was already up and pulling her clothes on.

She yawned and turned to him saying, "I heard a few mutterings from Carlos. I wonder if he is fit to travel today after his night of drinking."

"We will see." Tim quickly dressed and they went downstairs. Carlos was already at the table when they went into the room set aside for dining, but did not appear to be eating the food before him. "How are you feeling Uncle?" Tim asked.

Carlos certainly looked the worse for wear, and more despondent than usual. Rubbing at his unkempt beard, he grunted before mumbling, "If I ever decide to drink again, I give you permission to knock me senseless."

Chapter Eleven

Port Philip—Melbourne

The sun was almost at the horizon as they approached a small wooden church set amid the trees to the north of the town. Tim pulled his horse up when a man came out of the building and hailed them, calling, "Welcome to our town, strangers." Dressed in the plain black garb of a minister, he looked to be of the same age as Carlos. "Are you in search of a good night's sleep after your long ride?" As he spoke, he cast his eyes over them all, before settling on Jo.

"We are, indeed, sir." Tim dismounted and went to shake the man's hand. "Can you recommend a hostelry?"

"Most certainly. I think I was told at the last count that we numbered about a dozen inns. Just follow the road, and you will find one." He gestured to his right. "Choose carefully I beg you—it is unfortunate, but our fine town is being overrun with all sorts, and dare I say escaped convicts." With a shrug, he glanced at Jo again, suggesting, "Guard your lady well. Would she perhaps be your sister?"

"The lady is my wife, sir." Tim laughed inside at the minister's incredulous look.

"I do beg your pardon." He rubbed at his clean-shaven chin. "It is just that she looks of tender years—and her clothing..." Obviously running out of words, he gave Tim a wave and turned back to his church.

Tim called out a thank you, and they carried on. It most certainly had been a long ride. Eager to get this journey over and done with, the past few days had been long and tiring. Darkness had fallen by the time they were settled into an inn, with stabling of sorts for the horses out back. Although it was difficult to see much of the surroundings in the fading light, their final destination looked to be a higgledy-piggledy assortment of wooden buildings, some built along the main thoroughfare and a few set well back amid large stretches of bushland.

When they finally closed the door to their room, Jo said with a yawn, "I care not if the bed is uncomfortable. All I need is to wash the filth of travelling off my body and then to sleep beneath a roof and not in a tent."

Recalling the priest's words of warning Tim said, "Until we find out more of this town, it will be best to keep in mind that it is a fledgling colony, and therefore is populated by some rough sorts. Tomorrow we must find lodgings until we can either purchase a house or failing that, build one to call our own."

As luck would have it, the bed was not as uncomfortable as some had been along the road, and soon they were both sleeping.

Tim awoke to something tickling his nose. He opened his eyes to find Jo and Bracken staring at him. His dog let out a bark and jumped off the bed, heading to the door. Tim pulled Jo down and kissed her, saying, "Sorry Bracken, I have a wife to satisfy here, your walk will have to wait."

It was some time later when the three of them went down the stairs and outside. They hailed Billy who, as usual, was tending to their horses, calling him in for breakfast. Once they had all taken care of their personal needs, they went back into the dining room. Carlos and Gilbert were already there. "I have been discussing the likelihood of us finding suitable premises to buy or rent," he said as they sat.

"Aha, and what did you learn?" Tim nodded up at the serving maid, a girl of tender years but buxom proportions.

Carlos pointed to her, as she set bread, plates of sizzling bacon and dishes of oats on the table, saying, "This fine young woman has assured me that we need to see a certain fellow who will point us in the right direction. It seems that just a year or so ago, a shipload of migrants from Scotland arrived here and these folks were well skilled in all trades. Thus, we should have no problem finding labour should we decide to build our home. She also points out that most newcomers are doing just that, as they find it preferable to renting at a high cost." The girl sent Carlos a cheeky grin, before going back to the kitchen.

"I should like to live close to the river if that is possible," Jo said as she helped herself to the oats.

"Our first priority is to decide what we wish to do. We will have to seek out what business is most needed, and thus satisfy that need. Carlos and I are thinking of opening a trading store similar to the one Remy established, or an emporium similar to Aunt Sara's. Both are extremely profitable."

Jo stared at him, shaking her head with some vehemence. "Oh no, I have not come halfway across this wretched land to end up serving folk in a store," she said with a huff. "You and Carlos can do whatever you wish, but do not expect me to have a part of such a venture. Did I not tell you that one of the reasons I left Sydney was that I found the work in a store boring?"

Her heartfelt response startled Tim. "Then pray tell me, Madam, what do you have in mind? I for sure do not wish to run sheep as my parents have, and I do not wish to work for the government as I did in Sydney Town. You are no seamstress, I think, and you cannot make your fortune with your sketches—despite them being excellent—at least at this time."

That remark annoyed her, it was clear. "There are many other occupations to spend my time on. I will decide once I have seen what this place has on offer. And I might publish a book of my sketches some day." This last was said in clear indignation.

Obviously not wishing to be a part of this particular argument, Billy finished his meal in a hurry and rose, saying, "I would like to wander along the river. I have heard that two clans live in these parts, and I should like to see if I could find them. They have camps by the river. The horses are fed and have water at hand." Gilbert followed him out.

"I will go with them." Jo rose, and after sending Tim a defiant glare, turned for the door.

"Jo, be careful," Tim called. "Stay close to them and do not wander off alone." He sighed as she waved his remark aside and went out, followed by the ever-faithful Bracken, who glanced back at Tim as if awaiting his consent. When Tim said, "Watch her, boy," he scampered after her.

"You've always known she is a stubborn wench," Carlos said on a small laugh. "And I do not think you would want any lass who followed you around like a meek servant, willing to heed your every word, now would you?"

Tim had to agree to that, but was nonetheless concerned, heeding the words of the minister. Who knew what scoundrels roamed these parts? As he and Carlos discussed plans and costs, Tim fretted all the time while she was out of his sight. Of course, his wife was a woman of means and free to do as she wished with her assets, but he wished at times that she wasn't so headstrong.

Tim glanced at the clock that sat on the mantelpiece above the fireplace. Jo and the lads had been gone for over two hours and he was now beginning to worry. "I think I will take a walk and see if I can meet them," he said, as he pushed his chair back.

Carlos rose too, saying, "I will go along with you. We can take a look at the land on offer."

They had gone but a half a mile along the riverside when Jo came running towards them, Bracken at her side. She looked breathless and bedraggled, and the dog appeared distressed as he turned to look back along the river path. Tim ran to meet her and pulled her into his arms, as she moaned, "Gilbert."

Carlos looked along the way she had come, shouting, "What did he do? Did the bugger harm you? I'll kill him."

"No, no." She waved her hands. "He came to my aid when two thugs tried to pull me into the scrub. Bracken bit one of them on the leg and the scoundrel kicked out at him. I fear Gilbert is hurt badly." She dragged on Tim's arm. "Come, I think he is not breathing."

They followed her back along the path. Bracken ran ahead and when he stopped, they saw he stood over Gilbert's prone body. A pool of blood had formed beneath his head. Jo knelt at his side, and shook his shoulders, screaming his name, but there was no response. Tim pulled her upright while Carlos knelt and felt for a pulse. He looked up and shook his head, saying, "I can feel no heartbeat. I will stay with him while you run back and fetch the constable—if you can find one in town."

As they ran, Tim asked, "Billy? Was he with you when this attack took place?"

"No. He came upon a group of natives and was talking to the one I guessed to be their leader. I thought you might start to worry as some time had passed, and so Gilbert said he would accompany me back. We had only gone a short distance when these two wretches came out of the bush and began to follow us. When one of them grabbed my arm, Gilbert punched him on the jaw. Then the other one hit him over the head with some sharp object he carried and as Gilbert fell, the two of them ran off. I think they got scared when they saw blood spurting from his wound and forgot about me. They were merely youths barely out of childhood."

"My God, you will not go out of my sight in future, do you hear me? They were likely ex-cons. Perhaps on the run from the law." Tim stopped and pulled her round to face him, his hands on her shoulders. "Never wander off alone." He shook her.

"I hear you. I never knew…" With a small shrug, she wiped at her face where tears had mixed with dust on her cheeks. "I thought it would be safe here. I thought the minister was merely being cautious when he warned us of the dangers."

She sounded so despondent that Tim wanted to hug her. Instead, he said, "Come, let us see if we can find a policeman in town." All the while, Tim had visions of what could have been the outcome if Gilbert had not come to her aid. Lord only knew where the thugs would have taken her had they captured her. The thought made him feel sick.

It took a while to find the constable and then another hour before Gilbert's body was brought back into town. Jo gave the constable as good a description of the killers as she was able, but he feared they would likely never catch them, as they would disappear into the bush. He told them that there was a vast area of wattle and gum forests south of the river, and the men could vanish into the swamps, never to be seen again.

"It is unfortunate, but there are always ruffians who would prefer to steal from good working folk, rather than do an honest days' work for a living." After Jo explained that they were likely not more than fifteen or sixteen years old, he said, "Some lads have become so hardened by what they experienced as convicts they have no sense of right or wrong, missy."

When Billy returned later in the day, he was stunned. He and Gilbert had formed a strange bond of friendship. The clan he found could likely be of the same blood as him, but he said that he chose not to go and live with them, adding, "Now I know where their camp is I can visit as often as I wish." When they questioned him further, he shrugged, and asked, "Who will watch over the horses if I go?" Tim had a feeling he was so accustomed to life with the white folk that he felt no need to rush off to join his own people—people who even yet were penalised and slain by the newcomers. It could be that he felt safer with them.

The outcome of this tragedy shocked Carlos as much as Tim. Although he admitted that he never took to Gilbert, he kept repeating that he would not have wished such an end for the lad. Jo sobbed herself to sleep in Tim's arms after saying through her tears, "He was learning to say his letters and doing so well."

And so it was, they attended another funeral, and all plans were put on hold. Three weeks later, they purchased a large tract of land. It faced the river as Jo desired, but not so close that should floods be a danger in the future their property would be safe. Across the river it was as the constable said, they could see a vast area of trees. Within a fortnight, the hired men began building a two-storey timber home. There was ample grazing space on their land for their horses. Two men soon had a stable built alongside their paddock.

Some of the spark seemed to have gone from Jo, which constantly bothered Tim. She seemed to accept whatever they suggested without argument. At times, he wished she would return to the stubborn argumentative ways she had before the incident. Without being asked, the day they made payment on the land, she presented Tim with a substantial amount from her gold cache. When he asked, "Are you certain of this?" she nodded and left the room without further discussion.

Carlos spent many hours at the public houses in an effort to discover what would be a profitable business venture for them to undertake. Tim had an idea his uncle preferred the company of his fellow drinkers. He began to think that they had all changed substantially since starting out on this adventure, and not for the better.

The house was almost finished when Carlos said, "With so many new people settling here and so many houses going up, I reckon they will be needing furniture to fill those grand houses, just as we do. I have been discussing this with a skilled carpenter who is willing to offer his services for the right wage. This man built fine furniture in England and worked alongside his father until that old gent died last year. Alfred brought all his tools along with him from the old country and already has a couple of young lads that he is teaching his craft to."

"Sounds like a reasonable plan, Carlos. I am prepared to do whatever you decide would be most profitable. There is no reason that we cannot combine that with a trading company such as Remy has been successful with in Sydney."

"Right, I will go ahead and work out our first step. We need to find where to purchase the timber. Alf will ensure we buy wisely. I will speak to the man who was in charge of building our house." His enthusiasm was heartening. Tim was happy to see him with an interest that might bring him some way back to his old self.

While all the building was going on, they continued to return to the inn for their evening meal and to sleep. Billy was happy to take the horses back each night and return with them the next morning. Tim looked forward to the day when they would be able to move into their home.

Jo made a habit of sketching the local birdlife and animals while he and Carlos were busy with the men working on the house. When the weather was fine, she often sat beneath a tree, sketchpad in hand, Bracken at her side. Tim happened to glance towards her, noticing how pretty a picture she and the dog made with the sunshine glinting off her hair, when a small wagon driven by a man stopped nearby and the passenger leant over and beckoned to Jo.

Over the evening meal, Carlos and Tim continued to discuss the plans for a future business. Tim waited for Jo to mention the incident, and when she didn't, asked, "Who was the person who stopped to talk with you today?"

With a small laugh, she said, "It was a lady whose husband is in a position of importance it seems. He works for the Superintendent of the district. She told me they arrived here from Van Diemen's Land with the party of John Fawkner. After welcoming us to the settlement, she admired my artwork, and then was bemoaning the lack of schooling here. There are now three churches catering for worshippers, but as yet no school, and with three young children, she is despairing that they are becoming hooligans. When I said that although I was no teacher, I was capable of teaching them basic lessons, she was overjoyed. She offered me a weekly wage of nine shillings per week, if I would take on the task. She has engaged a tutor for her eldest son but feels the younger ones are not quite ready for a tutor." Her cheeks were flushed with her enthusiasm.

Slightly annoyed that she had not seen fit to mention such news before being asked, he said, "Well, fancy that. And are you interested?" She seemed as excited by this offer as Carlos had been and Tim was not about to dishearten her but did not like the prospect of her being out of his sight. Although there were already some fine people in town, there were still rogues and escaped convicts roaming the area in search of whatever pickings they could garner.

Her near escape and Gilbert's sudden death always loitered at the back of his mind. He drew some small comfort from knowing they now had a police magistrate, but the small contingent of police could not be everywhere. "And where does this fine lady live?" he asked.

"Have no fear, it is a short distance away, and she has offered to send her small carriage for me. I am quite excited. It will be good to pass on some of my knowledge. The children are twin boys aged six, and a girl of ten. It is the girl she feels needs a female teacher, especially one skilled in drawing." Her smile was radiant. "I got the impression that she despaired of my mode of dressing and offered me the services of her dressmaker as she felt it would not be proper for me to arrive at her residence dressed like this." She gestured at her breeches and laughed. "I welcome that, as I was beginning to wonder if there was a seamstress available in town."

"And when does she wish you to start on this venture?" Tim's heart was beginning to sink at the prospect of her not being with him daily. He had become used to her presence and having someone to argue and laugh with. Of course, he should have guessed that joining him in their business venture would not suit her—she had been adamant she did not intend to be a shop girl again. When he had tried to convince her that she would be more than a salesperson, she would have none of it.

Her excitement was palpable. "She will send the driver for me tomorrow." Rising from the table, she turned for the door, saying as she left, "I must prepare my one and only suitable garment."

Carlos laughed. "The lady seems to have settled in quite well. Have no fear, Tim, my boy, I wager she will soon tire of teaching three brats." Although he felt mean for thinking the same, Tim hoped Carlos was right.

As it turned out Carlos was very wrong. The first morning, she left a dejected Bracken standing watching her go, while she waved jauntily from the wagon—which was driven by a handsome young lad with a disarming smile, who climbed down to help her up into the bench seat. Worse, as far as Tim was concerned, her one and only gown was the one she wore on their wedding day.

As soon as the house was habitable, they moved in. While awaiting on the carpenter to finish making their dining table, chairs, dressers and sideboards, they had to put up with the sparsely furnished rooms. Every night in their bed, Jo went on and on about her splendid day, about how clever the children were and how well behaved. The mistress of the house had asked her to paint a portrait of her children, so she would require oils, brushes and an easel. Tim promised to send to Sydney for them, while each day he waited for her enthusiasm to wane. But with each passing day, it seemed to grow.

Thinking the house would hold her interest once finished, again he was wrong, as she seemed to be more interested in wondering what dress to wear each day, rather than whether the windows should have shutters or blinds. His adventurous explorer seemed to have changed overnight into a pampered miss, and he liked it not one little bit.

Watching Tim's agitation grow, Carlos commented, "She is young, and this is all new for her, Tim. You should remember she spent years around miners and rough sorts, and it is natural for a young woman to want to spend time with the upper class."

At least he was assured of her being at home each Sunday, but even then, he was required to accompany her to church, as her employer considered it appropriate for her to be seen attending the service, which bored Tim to the back teeth. Now attired each day in one of her attractive array of garments suitable for a governess, she seemed to Tim to be growing distant from him as each day passed.

"And what of the tutor?" he asked one cold August night when the wind whistled around the house and rattled the window shutters. “Are the boys at least not ready for his tutelage?”

“Oh no, Mrs. Wells insists that I am doing a wonderful job and wants me to continue. Even Cedric and Charles, the twins, are as eager to sketch as sweet May is. They are interested in the bird life that abounds here, as I am. And young Cedric has a rare talent for drawing horses in particular.”

Tim said no more. The next morning, he awoke to see Jo bent over the chamber pot, bringing up last night’s meal prepared by Jane, the excellent cook they had hired. “Are you all right?” he asked, placing a hand on her back as she retched.

Her face looked grey and gaunt in the early morning light, as she turned to him and cried, “No, I am not you stupid man. Do you not see that I am poorly?” She pushed him away. “This is your fault. I do not wish for a child. Why did you not take care?"

Tim gasped as the truth of what she said hit him. “I do not understand why you are so upset. Do you not wish for a child, Jo?”

“Of course I do not wish for a baby.” She wiped at her mouth with a fist. “Why would I?”

“Because it is natural, and the one thing most women desire?” He placed his feet on the floor and stared at her. “You are no fool, Jo, what did you think would come of our coupling over all these weeks? As I recall, you mentioned to me that Winnie expressed the belief you could be with child after one night together. If I thought for one moment you harboured these thoughts, I would not have touched you.” Now he was angry rather than disappointed. “What is wrong with you? You love working with another woman’s children, but cannot abide the thought of caring for your own child?” He stomped to his clothing and pulled his breeches on.

“Don’t you see? I am too young to be bearing a child. For the first time in my life I am experiencing what it is like to be admired and appreciated.” This she said with a stubborn pout.

"So, not only am I a monster for getting you with child, I am also accused of not appreciating you. And you are most certainly not too young to give birth to a baby." Turning his back on her, he pulled his shirt over his head. For the first time ever, he was so angry with her he clenched his fists in an effort to stop himself using this anger on her. Facing her, he said slowly, "There is another man. Is it this tutor fellow, or the young one who picks you up and shows such pleasure in your company each day? They appreciate you as I do not." He moved to stand over her. Bracken, sensing that both were upset, stood glancing at each of them in turn, his tail drooping.

She now had her face in her hands and mumbled through her fingers, "Don't be silly."

"Oh, I am the silly one, am I? If you recall I was not the one who wished to rush into a hasty marriage with you. I warned you the first time you offered yourself to me that a child would come of our coupling, but that did not seem to bother you back then. Truth be told I am possibly too young to be a father, but I would welcome a son or daughter to call my own, as any man would." He shrugged as it dawned on him that she had not denied she enjoyed the attentions of another man.

"Come, Bracken." Tim turned and stormed from the room. He went straight outside and found Billy releasing the horses into the small yard they had fenced off for them at the back of their land. "I will be riding," he said as he caught his horse. Billy said nothing but brought his saddle and bridle.

With Bracken at his side, Tim rode along the riverside, following it until he came to the sea. He pulled up and slid down his horse's side and sat on a small mound to stare ahead. Bracken sat watching him, his tongue lolling. "I'm sorry boy, I have worn you out," Tim muttered as the dog rested his snout on his knee. "What to do now? I cannot believe she would be so against bearing a child of mine." Bracken let out a soft woof of acknowledgment.

Tim had no idea how much time passed while he sat there. A small group of natives came along but when they saw him, they veered off in another direction. Nothing had worked out as they expected, even Billy who had been set on finding his kin, had decided against that plan. Tim often suspected he harboured an affection for Josephine, as he seemed reluctant to leave her. Carlos had come out of his doldrums now he had the business to concern himself with, but it was clear he was not as settled as he should be. He never spoke about Winnie or their time together, and Tim hoped that he would meet some fine woman to share his life with.

Tim sighed—then again, women often turned out to be more nuisance than pleasure. He never thought in his wildest dreams that Jo would harbour such a hatred of bearing a child. His Ma had borne another seven after him, and Aunt Sara another two after William and Jeremy, and as far as Tim knew, they loved having babies. Perhaps they were moody at times when their large bellies became a bother and their backs ached, but never once did he hear them say words such as Jo uttered this morning.

He rode back more slowly. After unsaddling his horse and setting it in the yard, he went into the kitchen where Jane was tidying up. "Do you wish me to prepare you something?" she asked.

"No, I will give Bracken his breakfast and eat later." He glanced about. The house was quiet. "Where is my wife?" he asked.

"The mistress went off same as usual," she said with a shrug. Around fifty years of age, Jane had come over from Ireland in thirty-nine with her husband and two adult sons, who were skilled woodsmen. They now shared a small house outside the settlement, and she returned there each evening. It was doubtful she had heard the argument earlier, but he sensed she thought his wife unusual for not showing an interest in their new home.

She looked at him with surprise when he asked, "Did you welcome your sons when you learnt you were carrying them?"

"Well, sir, at first I was not too pleased as I was just barely sixteen but, once that wore off, I looked forward to the birth of my baby. Doesn't every woman?" She came closer and peered at him. "Does the mistress not look forward to having her child?" she asked softly, nodding when he stared at her. "Ah yes, I knew but a few days ago, when she did not feel up to eating her meal." She placed a hand on his arm. "Do not fear if she says she is unhappy. It will pass, be sure."

Tim nodded, but said nothing, sincerely hoping she was right. The ache of disappointment stayed with him in the following weeks. They still shared a bed, but the intimacy was lost and neither made any move to restore it. Of course, Carlos must have noticed the coldness between them, but had nothing to say about it. He was still too wrapped in his own grief.

The business was fast becoming established, and soon their house was furnished with the work of fine craftsmen, and still Josephine showed no interest in any improvements. Although her condition was clear to all, Carlos did not mention her expanding shape. It seemed as if he was tiptoeing around them and escaped to the work shed adjoining the house as soon as he had eaten.

Tim began receiving stock from Uncle Remy, which arrived by ship, and the trading company soon flourished. There was a great call in the growing colony for furnishings and fabrics. He purchased an existing warehouse in town where the ladies could visit and buy such things as lamps to sit on the fine tables made in their workshop, or fabric for their fancy trimmings. Jo seemed happy enough with her painting requirements, but as with everything else, her enthusiasm had waned.

It occurred to Tim that as his marriage floundered, so their businesses grew.

Chapter Twelve

As Christmas drew near, at the table one dinnertime, Jo said, "We have been invited to attend the home of my employers for a celebration dinner."

Eyebrows raised, Tim looked across at her. Some meal times passed with not a word spoken other than those between he and Carlos regarding their businesses. "Why?" he asked.

She nibbled on her lower lip as she shrugged. "It is obvious that I will not be able to continue my duties in my current condition, so I suppose it is in recognition of their regard for me."

"I still do not understand why she expects our company when it is you they regard so highly. In all these months, the only time I have had contact with them is when I am forced to attend church, and then I have received barely a nod of recognition."

She shrugged again, obviously at a loss to understand his reticence. "It is the polite thing to do. I could not go alone, could I?"

"I do not see why not. You have had no qualms about going there alone for…" Tim counted off on his fingers. "…these past six or seven months."

She slammed her serviette down and stood, glaring at him across the table. Jane was midway across the room and stopped in her tracks, as Jo swept from the room.

"You could make the effort. Mayhap it is what is needed," Carlos chose to advise. Billy ducked his head and carried on eating, while Jane collected Jo's half-empty plate and went back to the kitchen.

"Needed for whom?" Tim snapped. "The wretched woman has been going back and forth there all these months and now expects me to tag along with her like a stray puppy. I will not!"

"One of you must make the first move. What do you intend to do when the child arrives? If she does not care for it, then it will need the love of its father. Perhaps she will change when she holds it in her arms. We both know she is stubborn, why else would she have followed you halfway across the country just to be with you?"

"It was not to be with me, Carlos, merely to escape her so-called dull existence with an uncle she despised, and employment she was bored with. I was simply the better choice—she has proved that. And now she has made it clear that she made an error of judgement by following me."

Carlos sighed, and Billy rose, mumbled something about the horses and went out. "So how is this ever going to be resolved, Tim? One of you must be the better person."

"Better person? Tell me, how would you feel if you thought the woman you loved was disgusted with the thought of bearing your child? She made no bones of the matter—merely protested that I had no right to make her go through this. As if it was all my doing. It takes two to produce a baby unless I am mistaken, and it is not as if I forced myself upon her." Tim rubbed his face. He always felt weary these days, more likely because he did not sleep well.

"Has it ever occurred to you that she may be scared? After all, she lost her mother in tragic circumstances, and then lost a good friend when Winnie died. I know she felt she could discuss womanly matters with her."

That was the first time Carlos had mentioned Winnie's name in months, and for a moment Tim was stunned into silence. He rose and paced about the room, before going out and up to the bedroom he shared with Jo. Darkness had fallen and the one lamp she had lit sent eerie shadows dancing across the walls. Bracken lay beside her on the bed, wagging his tail as Tim entered, and asked, "May we talk?"

She nodded, so he sat beside Bracken, stroking the dog's head. "Carlos pointed out that you may simply be scared of giving birth to a child. Could we be completely honest about this? The reason you gave me was that I had ruined your life and taken away your freedom—perhaps even ruined all chances of this other life you appear to have made for yourself with this other family."

"I apologise for blaming you," she muttered.

"Then please explain your reason for being so cruel. Have I ever done you harm? Have I ever treated you with anything other than the respect you deserve as my wife?" Tim raised his hands in appeal. "I have no idea what you expected of me when we arrived here. You must have guessed that I would expect us to work together and yet you made this decision to share your life with another family—and for all I know another man."

"Don't be so ridiculous," she said. "Who would look at me in this condition? I look awful."

"There you go again—so now I am ridiculous as well as stupid." Tim was not about to tell her that on the contrary she had never looked so beautiful. He went over to the window where he could just make out Billy in the stable below as he pottered about with the animals he loved. "Do you wish for us to be divorced?" he asked without thought.

Her response to that was a small sound of disgust. "All I asked was for you to accompany me to the home of the people who have been kind to me and hold me in high esteem."

"But even if I agree, it does not solve our differences, Jo. We cannot continue as we have. In a few months, perhaps two, you will give birth to our child. I refuse to live with a woman who has such a low opinion of me as to expect me to pander to her every wish and a woman who treats me with such disdain." At her small gasp, he turned and glared at her and then strode from the room, Bracken at his heels.

He opened the door to let Bracken outside and sat opposite Carlos who was sipping rum. He passed the opened bottle across to Tim, who filled his glass and gulped it down in one mouthful. Never a lover of strong alcohol he grimaced as he felt its warmth down to his stomach.

"Any better?" Carlos asked.

Tim shook his head and lifted his hands. "We solved nothing and said little of importance. I will accompany the wench to her celebration if only to see what like of people she so prefers to mix with." Tim refilled his glass.

* * *

Tim helped Jo into the two-seater buggie he purchased when it became obvious that she would not be able to sit upon a horse for a while. With just two wheels, it only required one horse to pull it. Billy held the horse's head until Tim took the reins and nodded to him. "Are you comfortable?" he asked, and she nodded.

Little more had been said between them, and when he told her that he agreed to attend this celebration with her, she simply said a meek thank you. She looked pretty this evening in a gown of pink muslin with white flowers dotted over it, and a bonnet purchased from a milliner recommended by her erstwhile employer. Her thickening body had required she order two new frocks. The night was warm with just a slight breeze. With Christmas just a week away, Tim had agonised over what to buy her as a gift—or whether to buy one at all, seeing as they still seemed at loggerheads. He hoped something could be resolved this night. She had ceased going to the Wells' house last week and this, added to her growing stomach, made her grumpy and unresponsive. This to such an extent that Tim was tiring of her moods.

He tried to put himself in her shoes and imagine what it would be like to change shape and feel so uncomfortable all the time, but failed, as most men likely did. Last week he asked Jane whether most women's moods became so changeable at such a time and she had assured him that yes, they did. “It will be fine once the little one arrives, you’ll see,” were her words of advice.

“It is the next house along here,” Jo pointed ahead. “Pull into the front of the house and their stableman will take care of our horse.”

Tim had thought his own house grand, but when compared to this one he now knew it was not. Every window in the double storey mansion was lit up, and there were even small lights about the door. Expecting a butler in hose to welcome them he was surprised when, as the young fellow who had picked up Jo each day drove their buggy around the side of the house, the hosts themselves stood by the door.

After introductions were made, Mr. Wells beckoned them over the threshold, saying, “Do come in. And how are you feeling, Josephine?”

“Huge and uncomfortable,” she replied.

After a manservant had taken Jo’s bonnet and gloves, they were ushered into a beautifully furnished room where at least twenty elegantly clad people stood or sat around, all talking or laughing. “Make yourselves at home,” Mrs. Wells said, as she gestured around the room. “Everyone will introduce themselves.” She wandered off.

A tall man of perhaps thirty years came towards them, extending a hand. With hair as dark and almost as curly as Carlos’s, he was just about the most handsome man Tim had ever come across, even more handsome than his Uncle Remy. As he took Jo’s hand in his, a frisson of fear went through Tim, as her cheeks went pink. Without being told, he knew this man was at the root of all their problems.

“This is Maximillian, Reginald’s tutor.” Jo pulled her hand free and wrapped it in her other one. She seemed fidgety.

“Call me Max, everyone does. So pleased to meet you at last,” he said, as he shook Tim’s hand firmly. “You are a very lucky man.” He had perfect diction, and a small touch of humour tinged his words.

“I am at that.” Tim took a step back. The man seemed to exude a masculinity and charm Tim found overpowering.

“You can leave your beloved here in my care if you wish to mingle.” He smiled down at Jo like a benevolent uncle. “They are good people.”

Against his better judgement, Tim did that and wandered over to where a butler was serving drinks. Once he held a glass in his hand, Tim went across to a woman who currently sat alone. After asking if she minded, he sat beside her and introduced himself.

“So you are our dear Josephine’s husband,” she murmured in a voice like honey. “I have heard good things about the furniture you and your uncle are producing.” Tim doubted she heard such from Jo. “I congratulate you.”

He thanked her and advised her to visit them, should she require any new products for her home. Something about her reminded him of Winnie. She wore similar attire and her fine jewelry sparkled beneath the many lights.

Her fulsome breasts bounced as she laughed merrily. “I am Celia’s sister, Monica. Are you looking forward to the arrival of your offspring?”

“I am—but I fear my wife is not.” He could have bitten his tongue, for that came out unintentionally.

She patted his hand with her fan and chuckled. “She is young. I guess she considers herself too young to be facing motherhood, but fear not, Celia assures me she has a charming way with the little ones, so will likely take to the child once it arrives.”

“Everyone keeps reassuring me with the same theory, Monica.”

“But you have doubts. I see it in your eyes. And a word of warning, she is captivated by someone who does not deserve her attention.”

Tim shifted in his seat. This woman was far too astute—and outspoken. “I fear we wed too hastily. It happened under unusual circumstances. She was willing at the time, but has since realised her folly, I think. She craves a life far different to the one I offer.”

"Tell me, you arrived overland from Sydney did you not?" At his nod, she continued, "And how did it come about that Josephine travelled over such a hazardous route with you?"

Tim made a steeple of his fingers, staring down at them. "She made the decision to follow me—and my Uncle Carlos, who was accompanying me."

"Would you like to know what I think, young man?" Her fan touched his hands again. "I think that all she wants out of life is some excitement. We all crave it. Perhaps she now feels let down to be pregnant at her age—and how old is she?"

"She turned eighteen at the start of our trip. She has an independent streak and has been brought up in an odd manner so is different to most other young women of her age."

"Odd manner?" Her eyebrows went up.

"Her parents were miners out near Bathurst, so she spent her early years with miners and rough sorts. When bushrangers murdered them, she was sent to Sydney to be under the care of her uncle, who had little time for her. So, as you see, it was terrible for her. From what I have been made to believe, her parents, although unusual, were loving. She had a teacher who taught her well, but this woman was also killed."

"How shocking. Now it is easy to see why she would crave a different life. Nonetheless, she is behaving foolishly."

"How so?" Tim knew deep down that was a true assumption but wished to hear what this woman thought of the situation. She obviously spent time with her sister's family so saw more than most.

"Well." With a knowing smile, she patted his hand. "You must know that you are a handsome fellow, a fine-looking young man in fact, but you are not experienced in life, am I right? Do you understand me?"

Tim felt the colour flood his face. "I understand you well, Madam."

"It is likely you have not even had a mistress—or at the least have not tasted the delights of many women apart from your young wife." She gave him a look he could not decipher. "You are at a loss how to handle this young woman who chose to marry you but is now seeking excitement elsewhere."

Tim felt she had gone too far but refrained from telling her so. "What exactly do you mean by excitement?" he asked instead.

Their hostess announcing that dinner was served interrupted her answer. About to leave her, he noticed that Jo put her hand on the tutor's arm allowing him to escort her into the dining room. "Would you allow me the honour?" He gave Monica his arm and she nodded as she rested her hand on it.

"After what you have explained, I can see that she would find spending time with the so-called gentry enjoyable and it is obvious she takes pleasure in their mode of living," she murmured. "But believe me, you need to take her in hand. She is young and impressionable." They reached the table and she said, "I see they have put me down the other end. I have enjoyed our chat." The table was set for sixteen. Jo was beside him, and the man Tim now loathed sat opposite, giving his full attention to a pretty, flirtatious girl who introduced herself as Miriam.

"Tell me, Maximillian, how long have you been in the employ of Mr. and Mrs. Wells?" Tim asked between mouthfuls. The food was excellent, with various meats including turkey, lamb and goose roasted to perfection, and an array of vegetables fit for any prince.

"Max, please," the Adonis replied. "I came from England with my employers and have been with them ever since."

"And did your wife accompany you?"

There was a brief lull in the conversation around them. The man seemed to pause rather longer than the simple question warranted. "I met her in Van Diemen's Land while Mr. Wells was engaged there." Tim heard Jo's small gasp at his side and wondered who else at the table heard it.

Certainly, the young miss at Max's side heard it, for she was now staring across at Jo.

"So, she is unable to accompany you this evening?" Tim raised his eyebrows.

With a shake of the head, Max said, "Unfortunately she is poorly after the birth of our second child."

Jo pushed her seat back, muttered, "Please excuse me," and left the table so hurriedly she almost tripped. One of the serving maids offered her a helping hand.

Tim glanced along the table and did not miss the nod and meaningful glance Monica sent his way. He excused himself and followed Jo. After asking one of the serving girls if she knew where Jo had gone, he found her in the garden.

"Are you unwell?" he asked as he sat beside her on the small bench.

"I do not feel well," she mumbled into the handkerchief she held to her nose. "May we leave please?"

"Certainly. I will ask for our carriage to be brought round." Tim rose, and placed a hand on her shoulder, "Is the baby causing you worry?" She shook her head, saying nothing.

Once in the buggy, Tim asked, "Is it me you tire of, or were you simply seeking the company of a man who is debonair and likely far more intelligent than your foolish husband will ever be?"

"You are not foolish, Tim, merely kind and too willing to please me."

He glared around at her. "Is not that what women want—a man who treats them kindly and panders to their every need. If my memory serves me well, you said as much early in our relationship." He shook his head. "I am at a loss, here. Do you not see what you have brought us to by your stupid behaviour? I cannot see where we can go from here, Jo. You wish me to change and I am unable to do so."

"Any more than I am able to." She placed a hand on his arm.

"But it is you who have changed. I am still the gullible fool who allowed you to follow him halfway across the land seeking excitement. You seem to have found what you sought, and it has little to do with me or what I want from life."

She began to sob, and Tim said no more, unable to find anything in his heart but anger. When they reached home, Billy took the buggy and Tim went in to join Carlos and the rum again while she went upstairs to their bedroom.

"I did not expect you back so early," Carlos said, raising his glass. "It was a disappointing evening?"

"It was a disaster." Tim shrugged. "My wife not only made a fool of me, but a fool of herself. Her inexperience has brought her to sorrow, and I fear we will never be able to cross the chasm that has opened up between us."

"Never say never, old chap."

When Tim finally left his uncle to his spirits, he made his way with some difficulty up the stairs, Bracken following him. His dog somehow sensed that his master needed him more at this time and had refused to follow Jo earlier.

She stirred when he sat heavily on the side of the bed to remove his boots, cursing as he did so. "I beg your pardon," Tim mumbled. "I did not wish to disturb you." He received no answer, which annoyed him as he was now in dire need of an argument. "Have you decided what you wish to do now?" he grumbled as he removed his breeches and flung them across the room. They landed on Bracken who had just settled down in his bed. "Sorry, old fellow," Tim said as he removed the remainder of his clothing and climbed in beside his wife, who he knew was now satisfyingly wide-awake.

"Just what did you expect would happen, my dear? Did you think the cad was going to whisk you off to a life of adventure that you were promised by your fool of a husband but did not receive?" There was no answer, so he prodded her back. "I can well understand you enjoyed your work with the children and can understand the attraction of working for the gentry, but what I cannot fathom is why you are so against having our child."

Abruptly she sat up and faced him. He could see her face clearly, as he had failed to turn down the lamp. She appeared to be angry, which pleased him. He did not wish to be angry alone. "It was nice to receive the attentions of a gentleman." This she said so softly that he barely heard her.

"A gentleman? I beg to differ. How can you call a man who has a wife and two babes and yet tries to win the affections of a young miss, who is too silly to comprehend what she is doing, a gentleman? He is a scoundrel who tried to hoodwink you." He glared at her. "And did I not give you all the attention you desire? I had a business to build and a house to build—all for you if the truth be known. And you expect me to give you all my attention. Good God woman, you are living in a world of childish fancies. I thought better of you, Josephine." His voice had risen. He heard Carlos stumbling to his room along the passage and turned his back on her.

A thought hit him then and he sat up again to face her. "Perhaps the child is his. With two babies already, there is no reason to believe he could not father a child. Mayhap this babe I am getting all the blame for is not mine at all."

She burst into tears again and thumped his chest with a fist. "Don't be absurd, of course it is yours, you are the only man I have lain with."

"Well, that is satisfying to know, but solves nothing. Would you like me to sleep in another room? We have two to spare—currently free of furniture, but that can soon be rectified." As he threw the covers back and prepared to climb out of bed, she caught him by the arm.

"No, please don't go. I am feeling low. Celia told me it is common for a woman at this stage of her confinement to feel this way."

Not to be so easily pacified he said, "But you have been low since the first moment you learnt you were with child, so that excuse holds no force whatsoever."

"I was shocked. I expected more out of life. I looked forward to new ventures, when I saw the arrival of a baby as ending my days of freedom. I thought my dreams of opening a school for girls one day, or making changes for the underprivileged women and children as Caroline Chisholm did, were just stupid ideas that would never come to fruition."

"You are still young and have many years ahead of you to fulfil your dreams, Jo. You are an excellent artist and already have been asked to paint portraits, have you not?"

"But none of these things can be achieved while I have a babe to care for, do you not see?"

Tim sighed. There was little use in arguing further. With a soft grunt, he turned his back on her and next moment sleep claimed him. It was still dark when he felt her fingers on his back, softly stroking. He turned and then she was in his arms. "It has been too long," he murmured before pulling her close and kissing her with all the pent-up passion within him.

She kept repeating, "I am sorry," as they made love. It was only in the light of morning when he awoke alone that the thought occurred to him that he still was not wholly sure of her trust, and was still puzzled as to why she chose to toss any love she felt away on a rascal who was so obviously after what she was not free to give.

* * *

"Merry Christmas." Carlos raised his glass and they all joined him in a toast. Carlos had made friends with the seamstress who came to the house to work on Jo's new outfits, and small garments for the baby when it arrived. A tentative bond was forming between them, to Tim's pleasure. Amelia's husband died on the voyage over from England. A quiet Cornish woman with a lilting accent, her fairness was a perfect foil for Carlos' darkness. She now sent Carlos a small smile across the table and Tim did not miss her blush as he nodded her way and returned her smile.

Jane, along with her husband and their sons, had also been invited, so with Billy, who had no idea what the Christmas festivity was all about, they made a jolly crowd.

In the days since he and Jo made the first step towards a small reconciliation, things had returned to some sort of normalcy. As she was unable to attend the Wells' house any more because of her condition and size, she spent the days preparing their house for the holiday festivities along with Jane. Tim could not shake the possibility that Jo was not, and never would be, completely happy. She spent some time each day at her easel, but even her art could not hold her interest for long.

Deciding to ignore his niggling doubts, he purchased her a gift similar to the one his Mama owned. One of her prized possessions, which she intended to pass on to her eldest daughter some day, was the necklace Pa gave her when she finally decided to wed him. Tim had written to ask Remy if he could get him something similar and it arrived on the latest ship to come down from Sydney.

When he passed the small purse to Jo, she looked up in surprise. Her fingers delved inside and when she brought out the pendant, her smile lightened her face. "It's beautiful," she murmured, as everyone present admired the gift. She held it out for Tim and when he fastened it around her neck, touched the pearl drop at the front as tears filled her eyes. "I do not deserve it," she said, so low that only Tim could hear.

"When I am very rich, I will buy you all the trinkets you desire." As he said the words, he wondered if a bauble or two would ever satisfy her craving.

Chapter Thirteen

As January passed and February came in, Jo fussed and complained as her shape grew and the heat and flying insects bothered her. Some of the townspeople had taken to bathing or swimming in the river in an effort to overcome the stifling heat, but Tim warned Jo against it, as he was sure it could not prove good for anyone's health. The population of the Port Phillip area was estimated to now be almost twelve thousand people. Unfortunately, a better system of removing wastewater did not exist, and still all waste, including chamber pots, from existing homes and businesses flowed down through open ditches and thus into the Yarra Yarra river.

A petition drawn up by Henry Fyshe Gisborne aimed to establish the area as a separate colony. It was rumoured that any day soon, Governor Gipps and the Legislative Council of New South Wales would establish Melbourne as a town in its own right.

All this was splendid news for Carlos and Tim. Both businesses were doing well. There was a ready trade with new settlers wanting fine furniture and all else associated with the new homes that went up each day. Tim and Remy kept in constant contact using the sailing vessels that plied the coast between the two colonies. Settlers arrived each week, and some were leaving the area of the town to seek out pastures to the west or further inland, so needed to take their belongings with them, much as his Mama and Papa did when they crossed the mountains years ago.

Billy went off now and then to spend time with his fellow natives but came back with sorry tales of the fights between the clans and squatters who wanted to claim their land as their own. Tim felt sure the white men would always win the battles as they had the rifles. More worrying was that the natives who did not die in these battles were reportedly dying of sicknesses previously unknown to them. Diseases such as venereal disease, smallpox and lung fevers like tuberculosis were becoming rife among certain clans.

When Tim learnt of these diseases, he sought out the medical man who luckily had decided to settle in Port Philip. This fine gentleman advised a fearful Tim to ensure his pregnant wife stayed away from the natives and that she and his entire household be meticulous about personal cleanliness. Sadder for Billy the doctor also advised that, at least for the foreseeable future, any natives Tim had in his employ should keep away from clan members he previously had contact with.

As February neared its end, Tim was about to leave for his warehouse when Jo called out. He went back to their bedroom to find her standing in the middle of the room staring down at a pool of water around her feet. "Jane," he yelled. Their housekeeper came up the stairs as fast as her legs would carry her.

Fear clouded Jo's face. He tried to comfort her as he and Jane coaxed her back to the bed, but she would have none of it, yelling abuse at him. Bracken whimpered as he glanced from one to the other. Jane shooed him out of her way, and he went to lie down at the other side of the room, head on his paws, as Jane said, "Hush dear." She gave Tim a gentle shove towards the door. "Now you go off and leave us to it. You can do little here. This may take a few hours."

"Hours?" Jo squealed. "I want this over with as soon as possible."

Bracken refused to budge, so Tim left him there, and as he went down the stairs heard Jane say, "Come now, my dear, it is all in the hands of the Almighty."

He took the wagon and with Billy went to the landing stage along the river, where he was expecting a new delivery from Remy. Loading the packages onto the wagon took his mind off his wife. What would he do if she did not come through this birthing? Billy must have seen his agitation, for he said, “She is a strong woman and fit. One of my kin was giving birth last time I visited them along the river, and she had a fine boy. This woman was not fit and not young. You have nothing to fear.”

Tim wished he could be as confident. Jo had not welcomed becoming pregnant and unless she delivered a fine healthy baby, he felt sure she would not contemplate going through the process again. Things had been almost back to normal in the months since Christmas. They never talked about her silly infatuation with the tutor, or her fondness for the gentry. She now took a little more interest in the house and was pleased with the crib that their fine carpenter produced for the babe.

Celia Wells and her sister, Monica, paid a visit soon after the New Year, along with Celia’s daughter, May, who said how much she missed Jo and couldn’t wait for her to come back to carry on teaching her. Jo’s response had been that she would be too busy with her baby and so her Mama would need to find someone else to give her lessons. The child pouted at that news, but it heartened Tim. They brought gifts of fine garments for the baby with them, and neither mentioned the evening at their house, or Jo’s speedy exit.

When they returned to the house after unloading the wagon, Tim left Billy to settle the horses and ran inside. All was quiet, so he sat at the kitchen table to read the letters he received along with the packages. He read the one from his Mama first. She was pleased the house was finished and the news about the baby and sent her best wishes for an easy birthing. She also reminded him that his Papa had helped with his own delivery into the world. The best news of all was that as soon as the baby was born, he was to notify them and she and Pa, and probably Annie, would come down for a visit.

Tim left the letter from Remy on the table and took the stairs two at a time. As he reached their bedroom, Jane came out with a pail and a bundle of laundry in her arms. “Goodness me, I didn’t hear you return,” she said.

He looked at her warily, unable to tell by her manner if the news was something he wanted to hear or not. "How is she?" he asked.

"She's fine and so is the little one. No problems at all, so I don't know what all her tears and fuss was about. She will have no worries producing a large brood."

Tim knew Jo would have plenty to say about that. "So, what is it? What is the little one?"

"You go on in and let your wife tell you herself." She nudged his arm and left him, chuckling as she went down the stairs.

Tim pushed the door open and stood just inside the room. Jo looked up and grinned. She nursed the little one and beckoned to him, saying, "Come and meet your daughter."

"A girl? We have made a daughter." Tears moistened his cheeks, as he went to sit on the side of the bed. Touching the tiny hand, he asked, "She is so small. May I hold her?"

"You may." She handed the tiny bundle to him, and the mite instantly curled her fingers about his little finger.

"She has my hair," he said, touching the fair mop, which felt like silk. "But thank goodness she has her mother's beauty."

Jo shook her head. "What shall we call her?"

"I would like her to bear my Mama's name if you approve. What was your mother's name? I have never had cause to ask."

"Yes, we will call her Isabella after your mama and mine was Julianna so that is settled. She can be called Bella, or Julie, whichever we decide."

Jane returned and took the babe from his arms, saying, "She needs her mother's milk, you run along now."

He left them and returned to the kitchen to read the letter from Uncle Remy, which held more good news. He and Aunt Sara also intended to visit once the baby had arrived. They would bring their youngest child, two-year old James. As Jo's guarantor, Uncle Remy had withdrawn her remaining balance at the bank as requested, so would bring that with him. When she had suggested such to Tim, he asked if she was sure, but she insisted she had no reason to return to Sydney, which pleased him. Always at the back of his mind was the fear that one day she might decide to return to her roots.

Tim set about replying to them with the news and then went outside to get Billy to take both letters to the Post Office in the hope they would catch the next ship heading north, so reaching their destination faster.

When Tim returned to the bedroom later, it was to find both babe and Jo asleep. Bracken had been down to the kitchen, mainly to be fed, and to go outside in a hurry, but was back in his position as watchdog. Tim patted his head and then stood over the crib in wonder. After removing his boots, he lay down beside Jo. She stirred and turned to face him, smiling sleepily.

"How do you feel?" he asked, as he stroked her hair, which had grown back to almost its former glory, and now reached just past her shoulders.

"It's a tiring business, you know," she muttered, then yawned widely to prove it. She reached up and touched Tim's face, which was now clean-shaven once again, saying, "I am so sorry, Tim, for all the trouble I have caused you. Will you ever forgive me?"

"All is forgiven. I hope you will love our daughter as much as I do already." He looked across at the crib when the baby made a snuffling noise in her sleep. "You have produced a bonny baby, my love, and I hope she did not cause you a lot of distress."

"Jane told me that the pain would be forgotten once the babe arrived, and she was right. She also told me that I owed the easy birthing to being fit and young."

"I know little on the subject, so have to suggest that she is the wiser and you should heed her advice." Tim kissed her gently, and said, "I have news—my parents and also Uncle Remy and Aunt Sara are going to visit us as soon as they are able. I have already replied to their letters so we could see them before the baby is walking. I imagine they will arrange to come by sea as I cannot think they would journey overland as we did."

"We were brave were we not, Tim? On looking back, I feel certain I would not have followed you had I been aware of the hardships to be faced."

Tim kissed her again. "I'm so glad you did, Jo, and I hope you have no regrets."

"Not the one. I have been a terrible person and I do not deserve you. You are the kindest sweetest husband a woman could ask for."

"I think not, love, but it is good of you to say so. I think we have both realised that there are many challenges to face in this life—it is how we face and overcome them that makes us stronger, does it not?" At her small nod, he continued, "Neither of us had to face the same trials as our parents. We are fortunate that we were born free, so I guess our challenges will always differ as the world we live in changes."

The baby began to cry, and Bracken jumped up to stand beside the crib, whimpering. "Have no fear, boy," Tim soothed as he rose and went to the crib, asking, "Does she need something?"

"I am not sure how many hours since I fed her last. I have much to learn. Perhaps you should call Jane, she will advise us. Would you please pass little Bella to me?" She sat up and held out her arms.

Tim went to the door and called out for Jane, then returned to pick up his daughter, who stopped her bawling and looked up at him with a question in her eyes. "I am your Pa," he said. "And I will always be here for you whatever life holds, have no fear."

Perhaps it was his imagination but the little one seemed to blink her eye in agreement.

The End

Please Leave a Review
This Author is
Counting on You

More Books We Love titles by Tricia McGill

Crying Is For Babies
Powerful Destiny
Laurel's Gift
Amethyst
A Call Through Time
Kate's Dilemma (Challenge the Heart Book 3)
A Heart in Conflict (Challenge the Heart Book 2)
When Fate Decides (Challenge the Heart Book1)
Amid the Stars
Maddie and the Norseman
Mystic Mountains (Settlers Book 1)
Distant Mountains (Settlers Book 2)
Remnants of Dreams
Lonely Pride (Beneath Southern Skies Book 1)
A Dream for Lani (Beneath Southern Skies Book 2)
Leah in Love (and trouble) (Beneath Southern Skies Book 3)
The Laird (Wild Heather Book 1)
Travis (Wild Heather Book 2)

www.triciamcgill.com
http://triciamg.blogspot.com
https://www.facebook.com/authorTriciaMcGill

2017 Bestselling Author
Tricia McGill

Award winning author Tricia McGill was born in London, England, and moved to Australia many years ago, settling near Melbourne. The youngest in a large, loving family she was never lonely or alone. Surrounded by avid readers, who encouraged her to read from an early age, is it any wonder she became a writer? The local library was a treasure trove and magical world of discovery through her childhood and growing years. Although her published works cross sub-genres, romance is always at their heart.

Tricia's love of animals has always shown up in her books. Tricia devotes as much time and money as she can spare to supporting worldwide conservation groups and is passionate about supporting those who do all they can to preserve our wildlife for future generations, especially elephants and orangutans who seem to be getting the raw end of the deal even in this enlightened age. She also volunteers for a local community group that helps disabled adults and children to connect to the internet with provided computer equipment. When people ask what she does in her spare time, she is heard to ask, "Spare time, what is that?"

Lightning Source UK Ltd.
Milton Keynes UK
UKHW011914210819
348362UK00001B/113/P

9 780228 608530